Term of Love

Myrtlemay Pittman Crane

Heartsong Presents

To my husband, Richard, my most ardent supporter.

And thanks to Elaine Colvin and all the members of the critique groups who have smoothed out the wrinkles in this story.

A note from the Author:
I love to hear from my readers! You may correspond with me by writing:

Myrtlemay Pittman Crane
Author Relations
PO Box 719
Uhrichsville, OH 44683

ISBN 1-58660-803-7

TERM OF LOVE

All Scripture quotations, unless otherwise indicated, are taken from the HOLY BIBLE, NEW INTERNATIONAL VERSION ®. NIV®. Copyright © 1973, 1978, 1984 by International Bible Society. Used by permission of Zondervan Publishing House. All rights reserved.

All of the characters and events in this book are fictitious. Any resemblance to actual persons, living or dead, or to actual events is purely coincidental.

PRINTED IN THE U.S.A.

"Do I have something on my face?" Tyce used his napkin to wipe at his mouth.

Heat flooded Melissa's cheeks. She'd been staring at Tyce's mouth!

"Your mouth is fine." Melissa stood abruptly before she said anything else stupid. "Care for more tea?"

"Yes, please."

With her back to Tyce, she regained her composure. After all, he couldn't know what she was thinking. She reached for the teapot.

She hadn't heard Tyce move, but suddenly she knew he was right behind her. His arms came around her waist, and he whispered in her ear.

"You don't have to do this all alone."

MYRTLEMAY PITTMAN CRANE enjoys teaching workshops at writers' conferences across the United States and Canada. She has published short stories, Bible studies, and devotions. Myrtlemay lives with her husband of forty-two years in Washington State. They enjoy traveling and family times with their three grown children.

one

"Beverly, where would I find room in my one-bedroom apartment for Mother to stay?" Melissa Wilabee stood with her palms propped on the butcher block in her sister's kitchen. Leaning forward slightly and lowering her voice, she added, "Besides, Mother would never agree to such an arrangement."

"It doesn't matter what Mom wants." A pout marred Beverly's beautiful face. With a defiant swipe, she ran the dishrag across the already spotless counter.

What Mother wants does matter! Melissa wanted to shout. It had mattered all her life. She remembered the first time she'd heard the term "unplanned pregnancy," and she set her teeth in a tight clinch. She was the child Mother never wanted. And when she reached five foot ten inches tall, Mother's words, "At least you could have been a boy," cut deeply into her soul.

Melissa suddenly realized a truth: Beverly had no idea what being unwanted meant.

With a rueful smile, she recalled the name she'd dubbed her sister on Beverly's eighteenth birthday, Beverly the Perfect. From her sixteen-year-old perspective, it seemed Beverly was perfect—blond hair with a hint of red framing her oval face. It made Melissa's dark complexion and hair seem dull. Of course, they both had blue eyes, but the difference was long lashes versus stubby ones. Beverly was chosen cheerleader. Beverly made 4.0 grades. Beverly won the lead in the school play.

But most enviable of all in her sixteen-year-old opinion, Beverly had womanly curves in contrast to Melissa's slender, girlish figure.

"I'm not talking about forever. Just a month." Beverly's

voice cut into Melissa's thoughts. "Charles and I need this time alone. There probably won't be another opportunity for me to go along when the company sends him to England."

"You're right. You deserve this trip. I know it hasn't been easy taking care of Mother these last six months. Having her live with you must be difficult."

"It's not just Mom. It's that bird."

As though on cue the parrot in the bamboo cage began squawking. The volume grew, and he ended his discourse with, "Not now, not now."

Melissa looked at Petey with dismay. "I can't have pets in my apartment."

"You remember Sandy, the eight-year-old next door. She loves Petey. I've tried to get Mom to give the bird to her. It's not like Mom is attached to the bird. She never takes care of Petey. I've asked Mom to put the bird in her bedroom." Beverly shook her head. "She just says a bird doesn't belong in a bedroom. Obviously this is the perfect time to tell Mom the bird has to go."

Melissa could see there was no getting around her own responsibility. "Maybe I can find an adult day care willing to keep Mother while I'm working. She can't stay by herself. I can sleep on the sofa so she can have the bedroom." Melissa moved to the breakfast nook and slumped onto a kitchen chair. "The timing's rotten though. Fall term starts a week from Monday." She rubbed her neck where tension heralded the beginning of a headache. "I can't possibly take time off. As registrar, this is my busiest time."

"Mom can stay by herself for a few hours." Beverly placed the last of the lunch dishes, along with detergent, into the dishwasher and pushed the start button. "She only gets confused in strange surroundings."

"Yeah, like my apartment."

"Are you girls arguing?" Darlene Wilabee shuffled into the kitchen, leaning heavily on her cane. "I can hear you all the way into the living room."

"We weren't quarreling, Mom," Beverly said with patient resignation.

Melissa again felt the shock seeing how fast her mother's health had deteriorated. How could she change so much in the two months since she'd last come to see her?

"Bicker, bicker, bicker. That's all you girls do. Why don't you run outside and play?"

Melissa's head jerked up, and she looked at Beverly for an explanation. So far this weekend Mother had seemed lucid, although Beverly's phone calls lately had hinted at deterioration of her mental faculties.

Beverly shook her head slightly. "We're just talking about how nice it would be for you to visit Melissa in Seattle."

"What's Melissa doing in Seattle?"

"You remember." Beverly guided her mother to a chair and stood close while Darlene slowly lowered herself onto it. "She works at North Sound Christian College."

Watching her mother's eyes narrow, Melissa felt like she was being stared at through an out-of-focus lens. Then the veil lifted; she was back.

"Of course, I remember. You confused me with this talk of visiting Seattle. When Melissa wants to see me, she can come visit me here. She knows where I live."

Over Darlene's head, Melissa mouthed the words "What did I tell you?" But inwardly she winced. Her mother's words had been addressed to Beverly, as though she were too stupid to understand. *This isn't an effect of her disease. Mother's treated me this way all my life.*

૨૦

Sunday afternoon, Melissa sat in the porch swing, gently keeping it in motion with the tip of her toe.

"You out there?" The call was followed by a shuffle-thump, shuffle-thump as her mother reached the doorway. "Don't get cold."

"No, Mother, I won't." Melissa looked at the heavy sweater covering her mother's dress. It had been an unseasonably warm day, and the temperature still hovered in the low seventies.

"Mother, you know this trip is a marvelous opportunity for Beverly."

Darlene sat in the wicker chair facing the swing. "Bunch of foolish gadding about."

Melissa repressed a sigh. *That approach won't work. Nothing that's been said all day has budged her.*

"I don't know what all the fuss is about. Beverly can go traipsing off if she wants to. I'll be perfectly fine right here. I've taken care of myself for more than sixty years." Darlene, staring off across the porch railing, didn't seem to be speaking to Melissa.

"You won't stay alone in my house." Beverly came out onto the porch, slamming the screen door behind her.

Melissa hadn't realized Beverly was within hearing distance. She tried to catch Beverly's eye, but Beverly was ignoring her. It reminded Melissa of the stand-offs between her mother and her sister when Beverly was a teenager. *Why is it Beverly always argues with Mother, yet Beverly is the one Mother loves?*

"I have my own house, thank you very much."

"Yeah, and you'll leave the stove on and burn the house down over your own head."

They glared at each other.

Years of habit brought Melissa to her feet. The tension tied her stomach in knots. She headed for her favorite retreat down by the creek six blocks from the house.

"What do I do, Lord?" she asked as she came to the small stream and sat on the bank. A pair of mallard ducks swam by, and she wished she had breadcrumbs to toss to them.

This was her favorite summer spot as a kid. Wild blackberries grew along the bank. She remembered returning home with juice stains on her lips, hands, and clothing. The summer she was five, Dad had made her a fishing pole from a willow branch, and they'd sat together on the bank. The scene came back so forcefully Melissa wiped tears from her eyes. It was the only thing she could remember about her father, except the bitter things her mother told her.

Darlene had confronted the two young girls as they sat at the kitchen table eating their supper. "Your father has decided he doesn't want anything to do with us. He's left."

"Daddy'll be back." Melissa's confidence never wavered. Day after day she took her fishing pole to the creek bank and waited.

Now, having celebrated her thirty-first birthday only weeks ago, she looked at the rushing water and realized how dangerous it was for a five-year-old to be alone by the river. *Had Mother known where I was? Didn't she care?*

It was surprising how little Turner, Oregon, had changed in twenty-five years. The new suburb where Beverly lived had sprouted up, but the old part of town with the house she'd grown up in remained the same. "How can it still hurt so much, Lord? Will I ever forgive him?"

She remembered the summer day when she was eight. In a fit of anger she broke the willow pole and shouted at the creek that ran through town: "I don't care if you never come back!"

He never did.

"I've tried to forgive him. I know all the psychobabble. I can help others overcome their anger and grief. Lord, why can't I?"

❧

Monday morning Melissa pushed the last of her belongings into the suitcase. She glanced around the room to see if anything remained.

Beverly tapped on the open door. "We'll bring Mom up in two weeks."

Melissa nodded. She couldn't think of any alternatives. Neither of them could afford to put Mother into a nursing home. And Mother had never been one to save for a rainy day.

"Just what does the doctor say about Mother?" Melissa had meant to talk to Beverly earlier but the time never seemed right.

"It's dementia. They're not calling it Alzheimer's. And the trouble walking is Parkinson's. They have her on medication, but it doesn't seem to help much. The doctor says it should keep her calm, although we can still expect times of great agitation. Sometimes you'd never know anything was wrong with her mind. Then she'll say the strangest things."

"Isn't there any medication they can give her to make her better? She's not old. Not even seventy yet."

"No. She'll just have a progressive decline in mental ability."

"What do you do when she gets agitated?"

"Mostly she walks around mumbling to herself, and there isn't anything you can do."

"She may forgive you for sending her to Seattle by the time you get back." Melissa picked up the suitcase. "On the other hand, I doubt she'll ever forgive me."

two

Melissa got down on her hands and knees and looked under the bed. She knew the pair of shoes wouldn't be there, but she looked anyway. *What did I do with them yesterday when I finished rearranging the closet?*

She looked around the bedroom. Almost everything that said "this room belongs to Melissa" was gone. Well, it had to be. Mother wouldn't appreciate her collection of Snoopy posters or the dozen stuffed toys from the Peanuts collection. After wrestling with the decision most of last Friday night, Melissa came to terms with the idea of overhauling her room.

The one exception to the complete revamping was her three-foot Snoopy plush toy. He just wouldn't fit into her storage unit. Everything else, she figured she could do without for a month. Stacking boxes as high as she could reach, she stuffed her belongings away.

She looked at the clock and gasped. "Seven forty-five!" The black flats would have to do. She couldn't spend any more time looking for the wayward shoes.

Wind off Puget Sound gusted in the morning chill, tossing drizzly rain into Melissa's face. Trying to avoid a puddle, she misstepped, and the resulting splash sent dirty rivulets racing down her nylons and into the black flats.

She hurried up the administration building steps. *Of all the days for Seattle to have a real deluge, why does it have to be today? The freshmen will be lining up at my office to receive their registration packets in less than half an hour. There isn't time to go back and change clothes. And could I find anything to change into if I did?*

She pushed open the outside door with a hint of irritation

11

and dashed through. Momentum hurtled her into the path of a man coming out of the president's office. She barreled into him. With wet shoes skidding on the tiles and arms flailing, she landed in a heap. Sheets of paper floated down around her like giant snowflakes.

"Anything broken?" The stranger leaned over her in a solicitous manner.

Melissa rubbed her knee. She'd have a nasty bruise by tonight, but it didn't feel broken. "I seem to be in one piece."

"Good." In one motion, he picked her up and set her on her feet. "Steady?"

She felt anything but steady. But she couldn't stand there in the hall with a stranger holding her up. "I'm fine. Thank you."

She tried to straighten her skirt, but it clung wetly to her legs. A drop of water rolled off her bangs, landed on the bridge of her nose, and slid to the end, where it trembled indecisively. She closed her eyes. What a mess! She reached for her nose then halted as she felt a warm hand wipe away the droplet. Her eyelids flew open. The most charming smile greeted her, and a pair of dark brown eyes looked into hers. She couldn't look away.

"Miss Wilabee." The approaching student broke the spell. "There's a foul-up with the gym. The team's supposed to have it for practice this afternoon. Now the dean tells me something else is scheduled. They can't do that. We need the practice."

"I'll look into it. But now I have to get to my office to begin registration." *Thank you, Carol. Your timing was perfect.*

The man still stood by her side, but she refused to make eye contact again. Melissa took a step backward and heard the rustle of paper. She glanced down at the tiles, where sheets of white paper lay soaking up dirty blotches of water. "Oh, look what I've done!" She bent down to gather up the papers and shuffle them into a pile.

He was beside her, down on one knee. As they reached for the same elusive paper, their hands brushed. "This is no big deal." His bass voice struck a chord in Melissa's heart. "Nothing here's been ruined," he assured her.

She held out the bedraggled sheets. "I'm terribly sorry."

He stood and took the offered papers. The right corner of his mouth tipped up in a lopsided grin. "Maybe if they're unreadable, I won't have to do all this work."

She couldn't help smiling back. Another drop of water started down her forehead from the wet strands of hair. She swiped at it. "If you'll excuse me, I must dry off." She hurried to the stairs at the end of the hall and made her escape.

"What happened to you? You're soaked!" Nancy Olson, the academic secretary, surveyed her as she stepped into the washroom. Her graying hair curled around her face like a halo.

"I started from my apartment in a light sprinkle. You know, the usual September moisture. But halfway down the block the skies opened." Melissa finished drying her face with a paper towel. "Look at this." She raised the hem of her broomstick skirt to show the brown streaks left from the mud puddle. "And my hair." The glance in the mirror showed black hair plastered to her scalp. "A lot of good it did to use the curling iron this morning."

"Hey, I have a hair dryer in my office," Nancy said. "Would you like to use it?"

"That would be great. Is there any contingency you're not prepared for?"

"Oh, I hope not. Back in a sec." In less than a minute Nancy returned.

Melissa marveled that someone who looked so much like a cuddly grandmother could be so efficient and put out perfect copy at 120 words per minute.

"Anything else I can do for you?"

"No, thanks. This will have to do for now. I'll dry off a bit and hope to get to my office before the freshmen descend on me."

"How'd your vacation go?"

Melissa paused, the plug to the dryer in her hand.

"That good, huh?" Nancy's questioning look made Melissa grin.

"Mother's not doing well."

"It's good you have Beverly to take care of her."

"Beverly's going to England. Mother's coming to stay with me."

Nancy's arched eyebrows shot up under her bangs. "In your dinky apartment?"

Melissa nodded. "I'll bring this back to your office when I'm finished." Melissa waved the dryer as Nancy stepped out the door.

"By the way," Nancy said, sticking her head back in. "Have you met Tyce Nelson, the new business manager?"

"No. Is he on campus now?"

"Yes. Dr. Allen's been introducing him around. You can't miss him. He's built like a tank. Must be those years he played soccer."

The image of smiling brown eyes flashed before Melissa. "Does he have blond hair and dark brown eyes?"

"Yes. I thought you hadn't met him."

"I'll retract that statement. Let's just say we haven't been formally introduced." Melissa turned on the dryer, bent, and flipped her hair over her head. *You're so right. I couldn't miss him.*

When she felt presentable, Melissa raced to her office. She had the new students' packets stacked on a table and her forms strewn haphazardly on her desk when the office door opened.

Ready or not, here they come. She looked up, but instead of students she saw Tyce Nelson's smiling face.

"Miss Wilabee? I'm Tyson Nelson." He stretched his hand across the desk and shook hers. "My friends call me Tyce."

"Welcome to NSCC. I need to apologize for crashing into you earlier. I felt a bit shaken and rather foolish. I'm afraid I didn't even thank you properly for your assistance."

"Are you all right now?"

"I'll probably have a couple bruises, but, yes, I'm fine."

"I noticed you were limping a bit on your right foot as you went up the stairs."

It gave Melissa a strange feeling to know that he had watched her walk the length of the hall and up the stairs. "I just landed on the right knee a little hard. That's where one of those bruises will show up."

"Sure you don't need to have a doctor check it out?"

Melissa shook her head. His concern was so obvious she was almost embarrassed. She hadn't done any real damage, only to her pride.

Melissa looked at Tyce's broad shoulders and strong chest and had to agree with Nancy's description. His navy blue knit shirt showed off both to advantage. She remembered how effortlessly he'd lifted her from the floor. The total package was charming: sparkling brown eyes; honey blond hair; full, smiling lips. A most kissable mouth.

She dropped her gaze to the papers on her desk. She hoped her thoughts didn't show on her face. She felt a red flush creep up her neck. "What can I do for you?"

"Nancy in the academic office needs a registration—"

"I knew it."

"You already knew she needed a registration packet?"

She shook her head. She should have known from the look in Nancy's eyes. Nancy was up to matchmaking again. Since when did you send the business manager to pick up paperwork?

"No, excuse me for interrupting. You say Nancy needs a packet?"

"Yes. A kid just dropped in off the street wanting to register. She's busy, so I volunteered to come get it for her."

"That happens so often I don't know why I'm surprised each time. People think they can come in the day of registration and be enrolled. No transcripts, no references, no reserved housing." She reached into her files and pulled out the necessary papers. "Don't mind me. This day hasn't gotten off to a very good start." She handed him the papers.

"On the contrary. Any day I make a new friend has to be a good day."

She looked into his smiling brown eyes and almost agreed.

≈

Tyce Nelson rolled over and squinted at the clock. The illuminated red numbers said two A.M. Groaning, he pulled the covers up around his chin and willed his mind to turn off.

There were a number of changes he wanted to make to the business office. He'd written some down but kept thinking of others. The filing cabinets would be more accessible if they were against the left wall instead of crowded between the door and desk.

Just when he figured he could put his mind at rest, Melissa Wilabee intruded into his thoughts again. When he'd picked her up off the floor and set her on her feet, he'd been surprised to see her eyes almost on a level with his own. He liked that. Small women made him feel like an oaf. Of course Melissa was slender, almost boyishly so, but still he found her appealing.

Whoa! Don't go there, Tyce. He twisted and gave his pillow a good thumping. *If I'd been a bit quicker, I could have kept her from falling.*

But his mind had been on all the information he'd just received from the college president. This new job wasn't going to be easy. Running the business office of a nonprofit organization never was. Depending on financial support from churches and individuals was an iffy proposition.

He was tackling this new opportunity not just as a job but also as a ministry. If enthusiasm counted, he figured he'd make a good showing.

His mind switched back to Melissa, and he wondered what she thought when he made the comment about a good day being one in which he's met a new friend. He said it before giving any consideration to how it would sound. Corny. What did it matter? He didn't need to impress Miss Wilabee anyway.

The poor pillow received a few more blows just for good measure.

three

Melissa opened the oven door, and the aroma of baking lasagna filled the apartment. The timer said it would be ready in twenty minutes, and Beverly and Mother hadn't shown up yet.

She left the kitchen, walked to the bedroom, and surveyed the bare walls staring back at her. She'd purchased a plastic storage unit on wheels and emptied the chest of drawers' contents into the new container. The unit fit behind the chair in the corner of the living room. She told herself no one would notice it there, especially after she draped a scarf over it and set a silver candleholder on top. Her clothes from the bedroom closet hung in the entryway coat closet.

With a nod of satisfaction she returned to the kitchen. The small cooking area opened to the living room across a tiled countertop. The window at the far side of the living room opened onto a grassy area with flowerbeds.

The maintenance man kept the grass mowed but never weeded around the flowers. After complaining to management a couple of times, Melissa gave up and spent an hour each Saturday weeding the beds. Actually, she enjoyed the gardening, and when she quit grumbling she found it a great source of relaxation after being in an office all week.

She was still gazing at fall chrysanthemums when the doorbell rang. Melissa breathed a silent prayer as she hurried to answer the bell. *Lord, this may be the most difficult month of my life. Help me to put Mother's needs first. Take away my anger.*

She threw open the door. "Welcome." She stopped, embarrassment coloring her cheeks.

"Surprise, surprise!" The male voice was high with a tinny

ring. "Guess I found the right place."

Melissa stared at the man in front of her. He still sounded like Gomer Pyle, and he still had the same scrawny chicken neck he had in junior high. "Gilbert?"

"Yep, it's me. Didn't know if you'd remember."

How could she forget? He'd been a source of embarrassment all through grade school. He'd lived next door and followed her around like a lost puppy.

"What are you doing here?" After the words were out, she realized how ungracious they sounded.

"I drove your mom. Beverly was just too swamped with packing for her trip."

"But you don't live in Turner anymore."

"I'm back." His wide grin showed a row of perfect teeth.

"Gil-l-l-bert?" her mother's voice called from the parking lot. Suddenly everything fell into place. Somehow Beverly had managed to avoid driving Mother to Seattle. She pushed past Gilbert and headed toward the loaded car.

"Hi, Mother. Welcome."

"Where's Gilbert?"

"I'm right here."

Melissa jumped at the sound of Gilbert's voice almost in her ear. He reached around her and offered Darlene a hand in getting out of the car.

Melissa took her mother's other arm, but Darlene shook it off. "I'm not completely helpless yet."

"Of course not." She watched as Gilbert led Darlene to the apartment. To her surprise, a tear formed at the corner of her eye. Now wasn't the time to get misty-eyed over her mother's rejection. Reaching into the car, she gathered her mother's purse and a small box that sat on the floorboard. Then she hurried after them.

"Here, Mother. Take this chair." Melissa pointed to a platform rocker she'd picked up at a garage sale and reupholstered. "Would you like a cup of tea?"

"Not now. Just bring in my luggage before someone steals it out of the car."

"Don't worry," Gilbert said, heading for the door. "I'm on it."

"Don't just stand there. Help the poor boy."

"Yes, Mother." Melissa's insides were churning, and her mother hadn't been there fifteen minutes. *A month, Lord? It's going to be the longest month of my life.*

Gilbert had the trunk open and handed her a medium-sized suitcase. "This one's not too heavy. I can get the rest."

"That's all right. I'll help. I see she's brought enough stuff to set up housekeeping."

Gilbert's laugh startled her. She'd forgotten the laugh. Kids in school had said it sounded like a mule braying.

Two more loads emptied the trunk, and Gilbert reached into the backseat and came out with another box. Melissa took it and trudged back to the apartment. The pile of stuff filled the center of her living room. Where was she going to store it all?

"And here's Petey," Gilbert said, coming in the door.

Melissa stared at the parrot in its elaborate bamboo cage as Gilbert whipped off the cloth cover. "Oh, no, the bird." She shook her head. "There are no pets allowed in these apartments."

Gilbert plunked the cage down in the middle of the table, scattering birdseed onto the tablecloth.

"You be careful with Petey." Darlene Wilabee rose from the chair, stepped close to the cage, and whistled a few notes. "If he gets upset, he'll molt."

"If my landlord gets upset, he'll toss us all out of here."

"It's been a long trip. I'm going to my room and rest. Where is it?"

"This way. Let me take Petey in with you. He can sit on the dresser." Melissa reached for the cage.

"No, no. If he starts squawking, he'll disturb me. Petey stays out here." Darlene looked around the small bedroom then closed the door in Melissa's face.

Melissa raised her shoulders in a helpless shrug. "Beverly said she would find someone to take care of the bird. What happened? I thought she was going to give it to the little girl next door." She looked at Gilbert, who just stood there with a silly grin on his face.

Melissa rolled her eyes. "Mother doesn't even like the bird. I'm going to be stuck cleaning the cage."

"Beverly said to remind you it's only for a month."

Melissa shut her mouth tight. Of course Beverly had known what an imposition it would be. She probably hadn't even tried to find another home for Petey. "It's against the rules," she repeated more loudly than necessary, then immediately felt bad for taking her temper out on Gilbert.

"Thanks for bringing Mother up."

"Sure. Glad to. I wouldn't miss this opportunity to see you again. You look great." The admiration in Gilbert's gaze made her squirm.

"I guess if you're going to get home before dark you want to be on your way?"

"Nah. I'm not heading home yet. Thought I'd stick around a couple days and take in the sights. Haven't been here in Seattle since I was a kid."

Does he expect to stay here?

"Do I smell something burning?"

"The lasagna!" Melissa grabbed the oven mitt and yanked open the oven door. The lasagna bubbled with a nice light brown crust. Tomato sauce dripped over the pan edge onto the heating element, where it smoked to a charred ember. "Good. It's still edible."

"Smells more than edible. Smells delicious." Gilbert peered over her shoulder as she moved the pan to the top of the stove.

"Bet you didn't stop for anything to eat on the way here, did you?"

Gilbert shook his head. "I suggested stopping, but your mother didn't want to."

"She'll probably rest for at least an hour. Let me dish you up some. Just sit right there." She pulled a plate out of the cupboard, dished up the lasagna, and set it before him.

"Won't you join me?"

His pathetic look made Melissa relent. "Sure, why not?" As soon as she'd filled her own plate, she sat across from him. He immediately bowed his head and waited while she said a quick blessing.

For several minutes they ate in silence. Gilbert finally paused. "This is marvelous, Melissa. You sure turned out to be a wonderful cook."

"Thank you." She searched her mind for something else to say. "When did you move back to Turner?"

"It's been a couple months now. I dropped by your mom's place but nobody was home. Didn't find out she'd moved in with Beverly until a week ago when I met Beverly in the grocery store." He continued to tell how he ended up driving Darlene to Seattle.

Gilbert scraped his plate clean and leaned back. "That was great."

"Would you care for more?"

His face lit up. "Maybe just a little." He pushed the plate toward her.

While he did justice to the second helping, Melissa learned more of what he'd been doing since high school.

"And how did you end up here?" he asked, scraping together the last of the pasta and sauce.

"Long story. I think I better go check on Mother."

Darlene Wilabee lay under a soft blue blanket, her shoes neatly lined up beside the bed. Melissa tiptoed to her side and watched the gentle rise and fall of her breathing. "I love you, Mother," she whispered before turning away.

Gilbert stood by the front door with his jacket over his arm. "I guess I better get going."

"Thanks again for delivering Mother safe and sound."

He nodded but made no move to leave. In a nervous gesture he began popping the finger joints on his left hand.

"Never did break yourself of that habit, I see."

"Sorry." He dropped his hands to his sides, almost losing the jacket. Still, he stood irresolute. "I wondered. . ." The Adam's apple bobbed up and down in his throat. "Would. . . you. . .and your mother, of course. . .like to go with me to see the Ballard Locks?"

His embarrassment was so acute it hurt Melissa to watch. He really hadn't changed since grade school. She realized he was still nursing the same crush. It wouldn't be wise to encourage him.

"Thanks for offering, but I doubt Mother would be up to such an outing. The Locks are quite a walk from the parking area."

Gilbert's face brightened. "I could rent a wheelchair."

Melissa shook her head. "Mother's too self-conscious of having to use the cane. I know she'd never submit to a wheelchair."

The silence following Melissa's statement was broken by a loud crash from the bedroom. Melissa and Gilbert raced to the bedroom door, and Melissa flung it open. Darlene sat on the bed looking at the remains of a milk glass lamp scattered across the rug.

"Mother, are you all right?"

Darlene raised frightened eyes to stare around the room. She eased toward the bed's edge.

"Don't get up, Mrs. Wilabee, you'll cut your feet on the glass." Gilbert grabbed a wastepaper basket sitting beside the nightstand and reached for pieces of the shattered glass.

"Careful! Don't cut yourself. I'll get the vacuum for the little stuff." By the time Melissa wrestled the vacuum out of the closet, plugged it in, and rolled it over, Gilbert had most of the glass in the basket.

A few minutes later, they all sat around the kitchen table.

"Hope that wasn't an expensive lamp." Gilbert looked duly sympathetic.

"Things can always be replaced. I'm just glad Mother wasn't

cut." Actually, she'd saved three months to buy the antique milk glass lamp from the little shop down in Greenwood. She'd almost cried at the sight of it lying in pieces on her bedroom floor.

"Are you feeling better, Mrs. Wilabee?"

"I don't know what that lamp was doing there. It scared me half to death when it fell."

Melissa gritted her teeth. Where else would you expect to find a lamp but on the nightstand?

"Well, guess I really need to get going now." He shoved away from the table. "Sure you don't want to see the Locks?"

"No, thanks."

"Locks? What Locks?" Darlene looked inquiringly from Melissa to Gilbert.

Melissa didn't like the expectant look on her Mother's face. "The Ballard Locks is where boats pass from Puget Sound into Lake Washington. This time of year it can be quite cold."

"I've never seen boats go through a lock."

"Melissa pointed out there's quite a walk from the parking area, but I can rent a wheelchair for you." Gilbert looked even more enthusiastic than Darlene.

"Mother, I don't think—"

"As long as I'm stuck here instead of back in my own home, I might as well see the sights."

"Sure. If you'd like to." Melissa felt like she'd walked into a time warp. It had been ages since Darlene showed interest in going anywhere. "How about tomorrow after church?" she asked Gilbert. "If you haven't made other arrangements, you're welcome to come to church with us."

"Sounds great. What time shall I meet you here?"

❧

Melissa settled into her chair, ready for the Sunday school class to begin. Gilbert and Darlene had been introduced to the class members, and people were settling down. Before the teacher could begin, the door opened one more time, and Tyce

Nelson walked in. He had the coordinated look, all in becoming shades of brown.

Melissa's heart did a quick two-step at the sight of him. All through the class hour she was aware of his presence a couple of rows behind her.

"Don't forget to introduce yourself to our visitors if you haven't met them," the teacher said as he closed the class. "Mrs. Wilabee, Gilbert, it was good to have you here. And, Tyce, it's good to see you. Tyce Nelson is the new business manager at NSCC."

Gilbert leaned toward Melissa. "That's where you work, right?"

"Yes."

The teacher closed with prayer. "Hope to see you all next week."

People rose, and the volume level lifted as conversations began.

"Good morning." The deep voice spoke directly behind Melissa. She wheeled to find Tyce grinning at her.

"Good morning. Tyce, this is my mother, Darlene Wilabee, and a family friend, Gilbert Reese."

"Nice to meet you both."

"So you work with my daughter?"

"We both work at NSCC, but I guess you couldn't say I work with her. Two different departments."

"You know she's single? Are you single?"

Melissa's checks flamed. "Mother, I don't think that's our business."

"Just general conversation. If he's married, I wanted to meet his wife."

"No, Mrs. Wilabee. There's no wife." Tyce was smiling as though he didn't mind Darlene's blunt question at all.

"Gilbert, why don't we ask Tyce to join us this afternoon? Don't you think that would be a nice idea? The poor man's all alone and new to the area."

Melissa watched conflicting emotions flit across Gilbert's face. The afternoon he'd planned to spend with her, he'd now have to share with Tyce. She was sure it was the last thing he wanted to do.

And what did she want?

After his momentary struggle, Gilbert smiled and said, "Sure. Tyce, we're heading for the Ballard Locks after lunch. Won't you join us?"

If Melissa weren't so embarrassed by her mother's behavior, she might have enjoyed watching the two men size each other up.

"Thanks. Haven't been to the Locks. It sounds like fun. Where were you planning on having lunch?"

Gilbert looked to Melissa. "Did you have any place special picked out?"

"I thought we'd just go back to the apartment and pop a pizza in the oven."

Tyce's eyes brightened. "Pizza. My favorite food. Tell you what. Since you've all been so gracious to include me in your outing, let me treat you to lunch. There's a pizza parlor just down the street. They have their big feast special on for just a few bucks. What do you say?"

"I really want to change clothes before going to the Locks. Don't you, Mother?"

Darlene scowled but finally nodded her head.

"Perfect. Gilbert and I'll pick up the pizza and have it back to the apartment by the time you ladies are ready. How does that sound?"

"Sounds like a plan," Gilbert said. The two men continued to chat as they walked ahead of Melissa and Darlene into the sanctuary.

They hit if off just fine. Maybe they'll entertain each other this afternoon. The thought should have brought relief. After all, it hadn't been her idea to spend the afternoon with either one of them. Instead, she felt ignored.

four

"Is that what you're wearing?" Darlene's expression of disapproval matched her voice.

Melissa looked down at her worn jeans and baggy sweatshirt and nodded. "The Locks aren't a dress-up affair. Besides, I hate getting cold, and there always seems to be a breeze there. I'm dressing warm."

"When I went on dates, you wouldn't catch me in a sloppy outfit like that."

"Date? This is not a date!"

"Of course it is."

"Then it must be a date between you and Tyce. You're the one who invited him."

"Oh, that was just to give Gilbert a push. He's been in love with you for years and just needs a shove in the right direction."

"Mother! I'm not in love with Gilbert. I don't want him pushed my way." Melissa's voice rose. Then she stopped. *Mother has only been here two days and already we're arguing. This is silly. Gilbert will head home and that will be the end of it.* "Let's just enjoy seeing the Locks, okay?"

Before Darlene could respond, the doorbell rang.

"Pizza man," Gilbert said as Melissa opened the door.

The aroma of cheese, pepperoni, and herbs flooded the kitchen when they opened the pizza carton. Bread sticks, a dessert pizza, and a two-liter bottle of root beer added to the feast.

"I'm starved. Let's bless this and dig in," Tyce said.

In a half hour they all piled into Gilbert's '96 Chevy and headed to Ballard Locks. When they arrived, Gilbert hauled the wheelchair out of the trunk. The sunshine took the edge off the crisp breeze, but Melissa was glad for the warmth of her sweatshirt, although she did feel a little grubby since Tyce and Gilbert still wore their dress slacks and sport coats. Darlene had donned a navy knit pants outfit topped with a camel blazer. A flowered silk scarf tucked into the neckline contrasted nicely with her graying hair.

The slow process of raising and lowering the water level to move boats up or down the canal didn't sustain interest for long. Gilbert took charge of pushing Darlene's wheelchair across the Locks so they could watch the activity on the fish ladder. Coming back, they waited for a large sailboat to move up a notch on its way to Lake Washington.

"Now that's a lifestyle I could get used to," Gilbert said. He waved to two children perched on the bow.

"I couldn't afford the mooring fees let alone pay for the boat," Melissa said. "Can you imagine how much that thing cost? I'd have to win the lottery to get one."

"What are your chances of winning?" Darlene asked.

"They'd be better if I bought a ticket."

Gilbert's bray startled into flight a couple of seagulls perched on the light post overhead. "That's a good one, Melissa."

Tyce chuckled.

Melissa couldn't decide if he was chuckling at her statement or Gilbert's laugh.

"I've seen enough." Darlene tapped Gilbert's hand. "Let's go. Beverly will be waiting for me."

Gilbert and Melissa exchanged a glance, and Melissa gave a slight shake of her head. "I think we've all seen enough. I could use a nice cup of hot chocolate too. Anybody else chilly?"

❧

"I vote for hot chocolate," Tyce said, then wished he'd kept quiet. He should head home instead of sticking around. Gilbert's feelings for Melissa were obvious. And although Gilbert was polite, Tyce knew he wasn't thrilled about having him along. How Melissa felt, on the other hand, he hadn't figured out.

Darlene seemed pretty transparent. She wanted Melissa to have a guy and didn't really care which one.

But what do I want? And do I want it badly enough to compete against Gilbert?

He watched the wind ruffle Melissa's hair as they neared the parked car. The sun picked up highlights and made the rest look even darker. Melissa stood ready to give her mother a hand as she transferred from the wheelchair to the car. But Darlene shook off any offer of help.

She's a feisty old woman. I imagine she's a bit hard to live with.

By the time they reached the apartment, Tyce had made up his mind. "Thanks for including me in your outing. It was fun, but I think I'll skip the hot chocolate for now. I have some papers I'd like to complete before tomorrow."

"Glad you could come along," Melissa said. It was polite but not at all as enthusiastic as Tyce would have liked.

"Nice to meet you." Gilbert extended his hand. "Maybe I'll see you again when I'm up visiting Melissa."

Tyce grinned. "Maybe so. See you tomorrow, Melissa. Good to meet you, Mrs. Wilabee."

❧

Tyce shut the alarm off at six A.M. With the move and the new job, he'd missed his morning jog last week. He thought about last night as he pulled on his running gear.

The paperwork took about thirty minutes. Then he sat in front of the TV not hearing the news. All he could think about was Melissa. Tall. Slender. Dark eyes that didn't tell you a thing about what she was thinking. He caught the glance she'd given Gilbert when Darlene mentioned Beverly. He almost bit his tongue to keep from asking who Beverly was. And nobody offered an explanation.

After he and Gilbert picked up the pizza, he'd been surprised when Gilbert directed him right back to his own apartment complex. He hadn't known Melissa lived only a half block away. While he was in Melissa's apartment eating pizza, he'd noticed it had the same layout as his own. Which meant it only had one bedroom. From what he'd heard from Nancy, Darlene was staying at Melissa's for a month. The apartment would be close quarters.

Tyce laced his sneakers and headed out the door. With just a couple days until October, wind off Puget Sound made him shiver. He'd need to pick up the pace to stay warm. He rounded the six-foot corner hedge at the end of the block and spotted a jogger ahead of him.

"Well, I'm not the only one out this early." His breath formed a plume in front of him.

Definitely female. The woman's long legs covered the distance in easy strides. A ponytail bobbed out the back of a baseball cap. *Wait a minute!* He increased his speed, and by the next block he was just a few steps behind.

"Good morning, Melissa. Mind if I tag along?"

She glanced his way but didn't slow. "Good morning."

"Do you do this often?"

"Four, five times a week." She headed up the hill to Phinny Ridge and Woodland Park Zoo.

ঽ

Melissa had heard the footsteps behind her. For awhile they sounded a distance away, then gradually closer and closer. When she couldn't stand the suspense any longer, she glanced over her shoulder. She knew the nervousness she felt was heightened by Nancy's warnings. "You shouldn't go out alone like that. You never know who's just waiting to find a victim."

In deference to Nancy's urging, Melissa purchased pepper spray. Now she felt her pocket and gave it a reassuring pat. Her action startled her. This was Tyce. She certainly didn't need any protection from him. She didn't need protection from anyone while he was jogging with her.

They reached the top of the hill in companionable silence.

Instead of slowing on the incline as she normally would, Melissa kept an even pace. She wasn't about to let this super jock show her up. Once around the huge parking lot then back home usually completed her morning jog.

"Are you up for another go round?" *Now what in the world prompted me to ask that?*

Tyce glanced at his watch. "Guess not this morning. But knock yourself out."

Melissa figured it *would* knock her out. She was already running out of steam.

"You're right. It is getting late. Maybe tomorrow." Silently, she berated herself for this childish urge to outdo Tyce. *He can probably outrun me anytime.*

She headed down the hill with a determined gait. Instead of keeping up, Tyce dropped behind. Melissa became conscious of her stride. She felt him watching her every move.

Never had the return trip taken so long. Finally her apartment came into sight and she unlocked the front door, slipping inside without a backward glance.

"Childish, childish, childish." Melissa stomped her foot in disgust after entering the apartment. "What's the matter with me?"

"I don't know. But you're sure being noisy about it."

Melissa whirled around at her mother's voice and collapsed on the sofa. "Boy, you gave me a fright."

"Your own mother frightens you?"

"For a minute I forgot you were here. That's all."

"And you worry about my memory? Oh, don't look so surprised. I know you all think I'm going batty."

The denial stuck in Melissa's throat.

"Where have you been?"

"I jog in the mornings. Sitting at a desk all day doesn't keep me in shape. I thought I'd be back before you got up." Melissa sniffed the air. "Something smells."

"Oh, my oatmeal!"

Before Melissa could reach the kitchen, a piercing alarm made her clap her hands over her ears. She yanked the smoke alarm off the wall to silence it.

Smoke poured from a pan on the stove, where three burners glowed red hot. In quick succession, Melissa grabbed a potholder, moved the smoldering pan to the sink, and turned off the burners.

As she reached for the water faucet, she saw that the dry oatmeal was charred to black flakes. There had never been any water in the pan. Steam billowed from the sizzling remains as the water hit the hot pan.

Melissa's eyes watered as she slid open the kitchen window to dispel the smoke.

"Must get this smoke out of here." Darlene's words reached Melissa too late.

"Mother, don't open the—"

The hallway alarm announced the presence of smoke.

Two apartment doors flew open. "Fire!"

"No! No fire!" Melissa assured her neighbors. But the automatic call had gone out, and five minutes later a crowd of firemen and onlookers stood in the hallway outside Melissa's apartment.

"I don't understand it," Darlene was saying. "Melissa was fixing oatmeal and suddenly there was smoke everywhere."

Melissa's mouth flew open to defend herself, but she snapped it shut.

Two huge fans blew fresh air through the apartment and pushed the odor from the building. In silence, Melissa listened to the fireman's safety speech. She ignored the shaking heads of her neighbors.

Finally the firemen packed up their gear.

"Are you all right?" a familiar voice asked. Melissa turned to find Tyce a step behind her.

She nodded.

"Anything I can do?"

To her horror, tears threatened to spill. She shook her head. An overwhelming desire to fall into his arms made her take a step backwards.

"I'll tell Nancy you'll be a little late."

"Thanks." She managed a teary-eyed smile.

To Melissa's surprise, a survey of the kitchen revealed little evidence of the last hour's chaos. The only calamity sat in the sink. She sank into a kitchen chair and buried her face in her hands. *Three days. She's just been here three days.*

"Are you going to work?" Darlene spoke from the doorway.

"I'll get there eventually. Guess I better get dressed."

"Shall I fry us up an egg for breakfast?"

"No!" The one syllable exploded before Melissa could stop it. She modified her voice. "I think cold cereal will be fine."

"That's really not healthy."

"It will have to do for this morning."

&

"A lot of excitement at your place this morning," Nancy said when Melissa entered the office.

"Yeah. Sorry to be late."

"Hey, don't apologize."

Melissa sat down at her computer and stared at the screen. She had reports to work on and a corrected line schedule to get out, but all she could think about was her mother back in the apartment.

Mother agreed to wait until I get back before fixing anything for lunch. What if she doesn't wait? I'll have to leave early just to make sure.

"Melissa?" Nancy's voice broke through Melissa's thoughts.

"Maybe you should go back to the apartment for this morning. I think you're too shaken to be of any use here."

"What am I to do?" She hadn't meant to fall apart but tears streamed down her cheeks. "I'm scared she'll hurt herself. What if I hadn't come home just when I did? A dozen families could be homeless now if that smoldering pan had burst into flames."

"Let's go to the faculty lounge for a bit."

Melissa yielded to Nancy's hand on her shoulder.

"This will do you good." Nancy handed Melissa a fresh cup of hot tea. The heat from the cup in her hands warmed her. Melissa hadn't realized how chilled she felt.

"Have you made any plans for your mother while you're at work?"

"I thought maybe she'd like to spend some time at the senior center. She does enjoy playing cards. But I haven't talked to her about it. She's only been here three days."

Only three days. It went over and over in Melissa's mind like a mantra. She didn't even dare think what the conclusion would bring. But, of course, not thinking about it only brought it to the surface. Twenty-seven days left to go!

"You'll drive yourself crazy if you don't find some solutions quickly."

Melissa smiled. She could always count on Nancy to get straight to the core of the problem.

"Go home, now. Take care of your mother. Reports can wait."

"Good morning, ladies." Tyce entered and headed toward the coffeepot.

"Good morning, Tyce. You're just the person we need," Nancy said.

Melissa eyed Nancy with suspicion. What was she up to?

"I'm sending Melissa home to get her mother settled. Why don't you walk her back to the apartment?"

Melissa's jaw dropped. "You're kidding. Why do I need an escort to walk two blocks?"

"I think you're still in shock from this morning, and I just want to make sure you get there safely." Nancy raised a hand to keep Melissa from speaking. "And to make sure everything is all right with your mother when you get there. You're not alone in this. We will see you get through the rest of the month. Won't we, Tyce?"

five

"You bet," Tyce said in response to Nancy. He offered his arm like he was escorting Melissa to Cinderella's ball. "You have a lot of friends, and I'm sure we can come up with a solution to how to care for Darlene."

"Thanks." She blinked back tears. "What would I do without friends like you?"

"Friends and the Lord can get us through anything," Tyce said, leading her out of the room.

A few steps along the sidewalk, Melissa removed her hand from Tyce's arm. "Nancy's quite the mother hen." She glanced sideways at Tyce. "I really don't need to be walked home."

Tyce kept pace. "No problem." He leaned over and in a conspiratorial whisper added, "She'll be waiting for a report when I get back."

Melissa laughed. She realized it was the first time since walking into the apartment that morning that she felt she'd make it through the day. Maybe she'd even make it through the month.

"Mother, I'm back." Melissa opened the door wide and looked around the room. Petey ruffled his feathers and trilled a couple of notes.

A peek around the corner showed Melissa that Darlene wasn't in the kitchen. "She must be in the bedroom." Walking to the door, she tapped before easing it open. Darlene sat in the overstuffed chair, a book fallen open in her lap. A gentle snore told Melissa everything was all right. Silently, she closed the door.

"Everyone and everything seem to be in one piece. You can reassure Nancy."

"Okay. Anything I can do for you before I leave?" His brown eyes searched her face. "Need any groceries? Garbage taken out? Dishes washed? Did I cover all the bases?" Tyce's smile made her heart flip-flop. The lopsided grin had a certain boyish charm.

"What's going on out here?" Darlene stood in the bedroom doorway, her elbows akimbo.

"I'm sorry. I didn't mean to wake you."

Darlene seemed to pay no heed. She walked toward Tyce. "You're Melissa's boss, right?"

"We work together," he corrected. "How are you feeling?"

"As good as can be expected considering my daughter's left me here."

"Well, this daughter hasn't left you." Melissa pasted on her brightest smile. "I thought you might like to play some cards this afternoon."

A gleam of interest lighted Darlene's face. "Is Gilbert coming over to make a fourth?"

"No, Mother. Gilbert's gone home. But I know where we can find a game."

"I better be getting back." Tyce gave a nod in Darlene's direction. "Good to see you again." He turned toward Melissa. "Take care."

"Thanks."

"Aren't you playing with us?" Darlene's question held a definite rebuke.

"Not this time. I'm needed back in my office."

"Well, what did you come over for if you weren't going to play?"

From behind her mother, Melissa shrugged her shoulders in a helpless gesture when Tyce looked to her for help.

"I was on an errand for Nancy," he said. "Bye."

"Humph! Even the good-looking ones are strange."

Melissa chose not to comment on her mother's statement. Was that all she was? An errand for Nancy? Despite a little voice that said the question wasn't fair, Melissa didn't let go of the doubt. She needed to keep a distance from Tyce. If she'd learned anything in life, it was that men couldn't be trusted. And that lopsided smile was too charming by far.

"Where's this card game?"

Much to Melissa's relief, Darlene put her coat on without hesitation, and they headed to the senior center. The woman at the front desk welcomed them with a genuine smile.

"Hi, I'm Mary. Welcome."

Melissa reached for the outstretched hand. "Hi. Mother and I thought we'd come and check out the place. See if there were any card players waiting for a fourth."

"There are three gentlemen over there who would love to oblige." Mary waved in the direction of one of the tables where a game of chess was going on. "Or maybe not now. You know how fussy men can get when you interrupt a chess game."

The twinkle in Mary's eye reassured Melissa that Darlene was in good hands.

Mary took Darlene's elbow and lowered her voice. "Let me introduce you to a couple of the other women."

❧

"I can't believe how simple it was," Melissa said to Nancy the next morning. "The woman at the information table was a doll. She took Mother under her wing and introduced her around. Mother found friends right away. She was as happy as I've ever seen her when I picked her up at four."

"The Lord does provide."

"This morning she was eager to go back. I think part of her trouble at Beverly's was boredom."

The day slipped away, and Melissa closed the last folder on her desk. She hadn't given Mother a thought all day. It was wonderful knowing she was safe and happy.

Tyce popped in just as she reached for her coat. "Everything going all right?"

"Splendidly."

"Now that's a glowing endorsement for any day."

"I'm off to pick Mother up. I'm still pinching myself that the solution to taking care of her is so simple."

"I didn't see you out jogging this morning."

"No. After yesterday morning I thought I'd get a routine started with Mother before leaving her on her own. I'm sure when she knows I'll be fixing breakfast at seven-thirty there won't be any more problems."

Tyce raised an eyebrow. "Sounds to me like you're in denial."

"What does that look mean?"

He leaned across the desk, his hands resting on the closed folder. "Your mother does have a problem."

"Like I told Nancy this morning, I believe part of her trouble was being left alone at Beverly's. Just plain boredom."

"Boredom can cause lots of things, but it usually doesn't make you set a house on fire."

"That was an accident." She pushed back her chair in such a hurry it rolled into the shelves against the wall. "I've got to go. She'll be waiting."

Melissa stalked home still grumbling to herself. "Just like a man. Thinks he knows everything. You'd think he'd be glad I've solved the problem instead of being a doomsayer." At her apartment, she climbed into her car and drove the few blocks to the senior center. A wind blew in off the Sound, bringing a dark cloud cover that made the day seem later than it was. She hurried through the senior center door to get out of the wind.

"Hi, Mary. How are you today?"

"Swell. Say, tomorrow we have a gal coming in to take blood pressures. You might mention it to Darlene."

"Sure." Melissa glanced around the room. "Where is Darlene?"

"Why, she went home at two. Oh, no." Mary clapped a hand over her mouth. "Don't tell me she was to wait here for you."

Melissa stood rooted to the spot. "Where would Mother go?"

"I have no idea."

"No, of course you wouldn't. I was just thinking out loud." Panic crept up from her stomach to her throat. *Where would she go? Back to the apartment?* "Mother has a terrible sense of direction."

"I'm sorry. We can't keep people here by force, you know. But if you'd let me know she isn't to leave by herself, I can usually manage it."

"It's not your fault. Maybe Tyce is right."

"Tyce?"

Melissa shook her head and waved the thought away. "Here's my cell phone number. If she comes back, please give me a call."

"Of course."

Melissa hurried back to the parking lot. Rain fell in dismal drops. The wind blew her hair into her face. She climbed into the car and slammed the door. Of all the dumb things. *Doesn't Mother know enough to wait for me?*

The motor started with a turn of the key, and Melissa revved the engine. Two hours. She could be anywhere. Okay. Start with the apartment. She fished the cell phone out of her bag and dialed her apartment number. After three rings the recorder picked up.

"Mother, this is Melissa. Are you there? Please pick up the phone and talk to me." Shutting off the phone she shook her head. *Mother's not in the apartment—she doesn't have a key. I'm going as senile as she is.*

That thought brought Melissa up short. She'd admitted what she knew all along: Mother had some sort of dementia. *First thing tomorrow I'll get a set of keys made for her.* She shivered and cranked up the heater. A key didn't solve her problem. She needed help. There was a lot of ground to cover, and she couldn't do it all by herself. At least not before dark.

The red light was blinking on the answering machine when she entered the apartment. *Well, of course. I left a message.* She hit the rewind button. It seemed to take a long time. Maybe

Mary had called. No, Mary would have used her cell phone number.

"Hi, Melissa. This is Susan. Please call me concerning the potluck at church Sunday."

"Miss Wilabee, this is Karen. Sorry to bother you. I was just calling to see if my student loan check came in today. Guess I'll catch you at school tomorrow."

"Mother, this is Melissa. . ." By the time her call replayed, the machine had come to the end of the tape.

She had to get help. Tyce? *No. I'll call Nancy.*

Nancy answered on the second ring.

"Mother's lost!" Melissa burst out. "What do I do?"

"Whoa. Start at the beginning."

Melissa fought the urge to shout. But she gave Nancy a brief account of what had transpired since leaving the school at four.

"Okay. You call 911. I think we need some official help. I'll call Tyce, and we'll round up everyone at the boys' and girls' dorms. We'll find her. Don't worry." Nancy hung up before Melissa could object to the plan.

Good grief! Everyone in school will know my mother is two pepperonis short of a pizza! Besides, do you call 911 for a missing adult? Melissa wasn't sure if it constituted a real emergency. She blinked back tears of frustration and anger. Her mouth set in a firm line, she punched in the three digits.

"911. What is your emergency?"

Melissa had barely hung up from talking to the 911 operator when the phone rang. She grabbed it. "Hello."

"Tyce here. Can you give me a description of what Darlene was wearing?"

"She had on navy blue slacks, a white sweater set, and her coat is a black/brown tweed. It's a long coat. Comes mid-calf. She always wears a scarf around her neck. I don't remember which one she had on this morning. But it would be colorful— probably have purple in it."

"Most of the kids haven't met her so I'm trying to describe her. Anything else?"

"Brownish gray hair. Oh! The cane. She'll be using her cane."

"I'll check in every hour until we find her. Each group has a cell phone, so we can coordinate the search." His businesslike voice softened. "We're praying for Darlene. God will watch over her. I'll be in touch."

"Thanks." Melissa wasn't sure whether Tyce heard her before the phone went dead.

"What's wrong with me? I haven't even prayed."

She collapsed in a chair and put her head in her hands. "Lord, I'm too concerned about myself and what people will think. Forgive me. Mother is lost, probably frightened. Watch over her, guard her. Be with those out searching. Help me to understand Mother and provide a safe place for her to stay while here. And, Lord—"

The sound of the intercom buzzer brought Melissa out of the chair. "Yes?"

"This is Officer Lewis. You called about a missing person?"

"Yes. Come in." She pressed the release button, then went to the door. A tall, gangly man in uniform approached. She ushered him into the apartment and offered him a chair. He sat and pulled a small notepad from his pocket. "Do you have a photo of the missing person?"

"No." It dawned on her how strange it was she didn't have a photo of her own mother.

The questions were a repeat of what the 911 operator asked. "How long has she been gone? What was she wearing? Why do you think your mother can't find her way back home?"

"Mother's only visiting, and she's just been here four days. Besides, she's never been good with directions."

"Wouldn't she ask for help?"

Melissa cringed at the question. "I'm not sure. She. . .she's had some trouble with her memory lately."

"Alzheimer's?"

"No!" The very word tied her stomach into knots.

"I see." The officer's voice never gave a hint of disbelief. "Do you have any idea where she might go?"

Melissa shook her head and whispered no.

Officer Lewis stood up and tucked the notepad back into his pocket. "You need to stay close to the phone and call this number if she should turn up." He handed her a card.

"Thank you."

Melissa paced the apartment. Petey sang a few notes of "Yankee Doodle" then hopped over to his feed dish.

"It's past dinnertime. Mother will be tired and hungry." She went to the kitchen and put a pot on to boil water for spaghetti.

When the phone rang thirty minutes later, Melissa grabbed the receiver. "Hello."

"Hello, Melissa." Tyce's voice sounded chipper.

"Did you find her?"

"Not yet. But we've talked to a lot of people, and several remember seeing her between three and four. Evidently she wandered from store to store, so she can't be too far away. I'm just checking in like I said I would. Keep praying. We'll find her."

The clock said 7:15 when the intercom buzzer sounded again.

"Yes?"

"Miss Wilabee, we found your mother."

Melissa punched the door release and flew into the hall. "Mother, are you all right?" She threw both arms around Darlene and hugged her close.

"Don't fuss. Of course I'm all right."

Tyce and a half dozen college students stood near the open door. "Come in, all of you." Melissa led the way and noticed her mother went directly to the chair she had claimed as her own.

"Before I forget, I must call the police."

"Why would you do that?" Darlene seemed upset at the

prospect. "I didn't do anything to call the police about."

"No, Mother."

"She doesn't look like one of the FBI's Most Wanted," quipped one of the students.

"I should think not. It's been a long day. I think I'll go to my room."

"Aren't you hungry? I made a big pot of spaghetti."

"No, I had a fine supper. Good night." She glanced at the group of students and headed toward the bedroom.

Melissa picked up the phone and dialed the number Officer Lewis had given her. When she hung up, Tyce and the kids moved toward the door.

"Guess we all need to get going," Tyce said.

"Where did you find her?" Melissa questioned.

"She was sitting in Harvey's Bar and Grill chatting up the customers."

"You're kidding. No, I guess you're not. What made you check there?"

"We just went from building to building. Didn't pass anything up."

"I wonder if that's where she had her fine supper. Say, would any of you like some spaghetti? I think in my panic I made enough for a dozen."

Tyce looked at the group. "Anybody in a rush to get home?" Heads shook.

By the time the students got up to leave, the empty spaghetti pot contained only traces of sauce, and Melissa had been filled in on all the details of the hunt.

"Thank you. Thank you all for helping to search. I don't know what I would have done without you."

Tyce ushered the students out the door, then stepped back in. "Are you going to be all right?"

"Sure."

"Why don't you bring your mother to work with you tomorrow? You know there's a mailing going out, and we can use all the volunteer help we can get. I'll bet she'd like to help."

"She probably would if you asked her." Melissa shut her eyes for a moment and shook her head. "That sounded terrible. Mother and I have always been at loggerheads. And I'm not sure why."

Tyce gave her a wink. "You get her to the administration building, and I'll get her to the mail room. Okay?"

"Okay." Melissa had said thank you so many times it now seemed inadequate. "You've been a godsend."

Tyce grinned. "I'll remind you of that."

six

"Going to work with you sounds like a nice idea." Darlene eased into a chair at the small table Melissa had set for breakfast.

"Good. I'd like you to meet my coworkers." Rather to her surprise, Melissa realized she meant it. And relief rushed over her at the thought that her mother would be out of harm's way for the day.

After breakfast Darlene went to get dressed while Melissa did the dishes.

"Will this be suitable?"

Melissa turned at her mother's question. Darlene wore a well-tailored charcoal gray suit with a rosy-tinted blouse.

"You look very businesslike." Melissa looked down at her own simple slacks and over-blouse and felt underdressed.

"I guess your young man will be there."

"My young man?"

"Don't be coy. It doesn't become you."

"I don't have a young man. I presume you're referring to Tyce Nelson. He is a friend."

"Humph! You never were too bright. He's in love with you."

"Mother!" The really good idea of taking her mother to work with her suddenly turned sour. Melissa held back the hasty words clamoring to be said. She breathed deeply and let the air out on a ragged sigh. "I hope you won't let Tyce know that you know."

"For now it will be our little secret."

"Good idea." Melissa felt sixteen again. *Say anything to keep Mother happy. But can I trust her to keep quiet?* A horrible feeling settled in her stomach. Not likely.

✌

"Nancy, I'd like you to meet my mother, Darlene Wilabee. Mother, this is Nancy Olson."

"Hello, Nancy." Darlene extended a hand in greeting. "I'm so pleased to meet Melissa's coworkers. How long have you been with the college?"

"Seems like forever." Nancy's cheery laugh filled the room. "Actually, this fall starts my twenty-second year. Can you imagine?"

Melissa noticed Nancy carefully avoided any mention of last night's search. She hadn't said anything to her mother either. Would everyone pretend it didn't happen?

"Good morning, ladies."

If Melissa's ear hadn't told her it was Tyce's voice she heard, the lurch of her heart would have.

"Oh, there you are," Darlene said, giving Tyce a wide smile.

Melissa's smile froze. Her heartbeat increased and panic rushed to her throat. She waited for Darlene to say something embarrassing.

"It's me, all right." Tyce smiled back. "Just checked in on the mailing project. Looks like it's going well."

"What project is that?" Darlene asked.

Tyce explained the college's use of volunteers to get out large mailings to the constituency.

Melissa gradually relaxed. Here was a safe topic.

"Say, when you get bored following Melissa around, you could come over to the mail room and give us a hand."

Melissa marveled at the seamless segue. There was no way Darlene could suspect this had been set up beforehand.

"I think I'd like that." Darlene looked around Nancy's office. "So which desk is yours?"

"This way, Mother. Let's continue the grand tour. My office is up one flight."

As they approached the staircase, Darlene paused. "Don't they have an elevator in this building?"

"Afraid not."

"Let me give you a hand." The offer came from Tyce, who'd just come out of Nancy's office. He proffered his arm to Darlene, and together they inched their way up the stairs.

Melissa followed, watching the difficulty her mother had in climbing. When did she become so feeble? A surge of guilt shot through Melissa. She'd stayed away from home as much as possible—even cut the twice-yearly visits short.

They'd reached the landing before Melissa paid attention to Darlene and Tyce's discussion.

"You realize, of course, that Melissa's had several opportunities to get married."

"I'm sure with anyone as lovely as Melissa, that's true."

"I know people today are putting off getting married until later in life. But if Melissa wants children she better not wait much longer."

Horror and fascination kept Melissa mute. How would Tyce respond to that?

Tyce patted the frail hand on his arm. "You mothers must all belong to the same club. I have a sister a couple years younger than Melissa. Just a few weeks ago my mother fussed at her. You know what?" He bent his head closer to the gray one beside him. "I think my sister becomes more determined to wait every time Mother brings up the subject."

"Rebellion. Pure and simple."

"I'm afraid so. I suggested Mom back off and let my sister make up her own mind. When the right guy comes along she'll come around."

"Humph." Darlene climbed the last few stairs in silence.

Melissa felt like an eavesdropper. *But they're talking about me, and they know I'm right behind them. Besides, what right do they have to be discussing my personal life?*

Suddenly Darlene spoke again. "You know, if you had a mind to, you could change her mind."

"Mother, I think this discussion is over." Melissa turned to

Tyce. "Thanks for the help. We'll be over to the mail room later."

"Looking forward to it." The mischievous gleam in Tyce's eye sent a surge of anger through Melissa. The man was enjoying her embarrassment.

"Here it is." Melissa made a grand gesture as she ushered her mother into the room. "My very own office."

"Not very big," Darlene said, taking in the room at a glance.

"No, but I like it." She went to the window and picked a drooping leaf off her favorite plant. She surveyed the room, considering how her mother might see it. A few Charlie Brown collectibles were interspersed between the books on the shelves. Her framed college diploma hung on one wall. It was rather bare. She'd have to spruce it up.

An hour later Melissa and Darlene entered the mailroom. About twenty-five people sat at the tables preparing the mailing. Melissa glanced around to find Tyce but saw only the mailroom supervisor.

"Hi, Melissa. Tyce said you'd be down." The perky brunette offered a hand to Darlene. "It's nice to meet you, Mrs. Wilabee. Thanks for coming to help. This group over here is collating. I could use you here."

Darlene followed the supervisor, and Melissa watched as Darlene received the instructions for putting the pieces together in proper order. A sense of relief flowed through her. She had been secretly afraid Darlene would put labels on upside down, get envelopes out of zip code order, or generally mess up. Collating seemed a safe task.

❧

Melissa glanced up and realized the morning had flown by. Mother would be breaking for lunch soon. She replaced two files into the cabinet before leaving her office.

The volunteer crew was already sitting down eating by the time Melissa reached the cafeteria. She greeted several regulars she'd come to know. "How's it going?"

"Zipping right along. About another hour's worth and we'll be done."

"Yeah. With a crew this size we get done in a hurry."

Melissa took a few steps toward where Darlene sat, then stopped. She was chatting happily with her neighbors, and there seemed no good reason to disturb them. Instead, Melissa joined the line of students and faculty picking up their lunch.

"Melissa, over here."

She glanced to her right and saw Tyce motioning toward an empty chair beside him. Nancy occupied the spot on the other side.

"How did your mother do?" Nancy asked as Melissa slid into the vacant chair.

"All right, I guess. I haven't spoken to her."

"She makes friends easily. I noticed her visiting with several of the other volunteers."

Melissa nodded then bowed her head for a quick blessing on the food. She'd hardly gotten past "Thank you for this food" when an inner voice interrupted. *She's a friend to everyone but me.* She hated the stab of jealousy that pierced her heart. She kept her head bowed for several more seconds while she fought to control her emotions. The prayer became a plea for help.

When she finally raised her head, both Nancy and Tyce were looking at her.

"I was thinking," Nancy began. "I'd like to have your mother over for dinner tonight."

"Just Mother?" The question slipped out before Melissa could stop it.

"Seems to me you could use an evening apart. And I really would like to get to know your mother."

"Only if I can swear you to secrecy," Melissa said.

"What?"

"I'm sure while the two of you are talking you'll find out everything I ever did."

"My lips are sealed."

Melissa bit into a meatball. Of course the cook would have spaghetti on the menu after she filled the kids up with it last night.

Just then a student stopped by. "Yours was better," he said.

"I agree," Tyce said.

"Thank you both." She grinned at the boy, whose blue and green spiked hair stood out at all angles. "But don't tell the cook."

"Don't tell the cook what?" Nancy asked. "Did I miss something?"

Tyce recounted the evening meal. "Ate every last strand of spaghetti," he concluded.

"Maybe you need an invitation out to dinner," Nancy suggested, throwing Tyce a meaningful glance. "Sounds like the cupboard is bare."

Tyce's eyebrows lifted in agreement. "Excellent suggestion. How about something Chinese? Or would you prefer Mexican?"

"That's really not necessary. I do have a few staples left." Melissa laughed in dismissal. They were ganging up on her, and her options were running out. "What I really need is just a quiet evening in."

"Perfect!" Nancy exclaimed. "Tyce, that new Chinese place has the best carry-out."

"Great idea." He turned laughing eyes on Melissa. "What time do you want to eat?"

❧

Melissa tossed a pair of navy slacks on the sofa. Pushing clothes aside, she searched the closet for a blouse to go with them. Since moving her stuff to the hall closet she couldn't find a thing.

She'd vowed she wouldn't get dressed up just because Tyce was coming over. The closer it came to six P.M. the more she wrestled with changing into something besides the jeans she slipped on after work. Finally she chose a burgundy pullover with a cable knit pattern to top a navy blouse. She slipped her feet into navy flats and surveyed the results in the mirror.

As she turned her head, her ponytail flipped over her shoulder. Reaching up, she snatched off the scrunchie and shook her hair loose. The black shiny waves framed her face, softening the high, angular cheekbones.

Melissa frowned at her reflection. Who was she kidding? There was only one reason she'd let her hair down—to make an impression on Tyce. Well, it wasn't going to happen. She reached for the scrunchie. It fell from her fingers, and before she could retrieve it the door buzzer sounded. Tyce would be standing out there with his arms full of food. She left the scrunchie on the floor and answered the buzzer on the second ring.

The unmistakable aroma of Chinese food preceded Tyce into the apartment. "You're lucky I arrived with any of this. The smell has made my stomach growl ever since I picked it up. Shall I put it on the counter or the table?"

"Table will be fine." She helped him set out the cardboard containers. The table setting would look prettier if she put the food into bowls, but she rationalized it would stay hotter in its original containers. Besides, this wasn't a formal meal.

"Pretty bouquet," Tyce said, laying out the packets of soy sauce next to a bowl filled with chrysanthemums.

With a grin Melissa agreed, poured tea into two cups, and brought the teacups to the table.

"Um, smells like Market Spice."

She looked up in surprise. "You're familiar with Market Spice?" She couldn't quite picture him as a tea drinker, even though she'd fixed it to go with the take-out.

"Must be the one-quarter Englishman in me."

They sat, Melissa gave thanks, and Tyce began opening the containers. "Does that bird sing all the time?"

Melissa glanced at Petey. "Pretty much. Although I'm not sure what he does could be called singing. Maybe squawking.

I've gotten used to him in the last few days and hardly notice anymore." She shoved back from the table. "I'll cover his cage."

"Oh, no. I wasn't complaining. My sister got a bird when she was in high school. No matter what she tried that bird wouldn't sing. I was just thinking how much she would have liked this one."

"I wish she did have him. What messy creatures birds are!" She watched a frown form on Tyce's brow and added in explanation, "Petey is Mother's."

"I wondered how you got away with having a bird since there is such a strict no-pet policy around here."

"Got-away-with is right. I told Mother when she arrived with Petey the landlord would throw us out if he discovered Petey. By then, of course, it was too late to do anything but hope he goes undetected."

"I don't know. He's a pretty loud bird."

"I seem to be breaking all the rules around here."

At Tyce's questioning look, she explained. "The last two days of rain beat the flowers almost to the ground. Coming home from work I rescued them from their demise even though I would have been angered had anyone else picked them. I guess I rationalized they wouldn't have been there at all if I hadn't weeded the beds."

He picked up the bowl and brought it to his nose. "They don't even smell good. Would be a shame to be kicked out because of a bird you dislike and flowers without a pleasing scent."

They laughed, and Petey hit a particularly high, loud note.

"This is really good," Melissa said after they'd scraped the last of the pork chow mein onto their plates.

Tyce leaned back in his chair. "So how are you and Darlene getting along?"

"Fine."

"That's the kind of answer you give the clerk at the check-out counter. I want to know how you're doing."

Melissa gazed into Tyce's face. Earnest concern shone in his eyes. "In my phone conversations with Beverly, she'd been complaining about Mother forgetting things. Like once, she put the milk in the oven instead of the refrigerator." Melissa shook her head. "But, my goodness, I forget and do dumb things. I never realized Mother really had a problem.

"The thing is now I know it's not safe for Beverly to leave Mother alone all day while she's at work. And it's not safe for me to leave her alone. I don't know what we're going to do."

"Do you have other siblings who can help?"

"No, there's just the two of us. And two was one too many." Melissa hadn't meant to say that. She recalled something a Sunday school teacher had said once. "If you think it, it's bound to be said sometime." The teacher had been referring to swear words, but the analogy applied.

Tyce didn't comment. He picked up the last of an egg roll and popped it into his mouth. Melissa's eyes followed the egg roll to his lips. They were probably the best feature of his handsome face. No thin miserly lips here.

"Do I have something on my face?" Tyce used his napkin to wipe at his mouth.

Heat flooded Melissa's cheeks. She'd been staring at Tyce's mouth!

"Your mouth is fine." Melissa stood abruptly before she said anything else stupid. "Care for more tea?"

"Yes, please."

With her back to Tyce, she regained her composure. After all, he couldn't know what she was thinking. She reached for the teapot.

She hadn't heard Tyce move, but suddenly she knew he was right behind her. His arms came around her waist, and he whispered in her ear.

"You don't have to do this all alone."

The temptation to lean back into Tyce's encircling arms almost undid Melissa. Then she stiffened. She couldn't count on men to be around when she really needed them.

seven

At the first sign of resistance Tyce dropped his arms from Melissa's waist but didn't step back. She smelled good. Perhaps it was her shampoo. The glossy strands of hair hung only inches from his face. He'd never seen her without one of those ridiculous bands gathering her hair into a ponytail. Why would anyone want to hide all this beauty? He forced himself not to reach up and tangle his fingers in the long locks.

"Any time you need help, call."

"Thanks. You and Nancy have been a big support."

Tyce smiled wryly. He didn't really want to be lumped with Nancy.

He returned to the table. "Come. Let's read our fortunes." He picked up one of the cookies. "I'm sure yours will say something about a tall handsome man." He forced a light note in his voice and gave her a roguish grin. He cracked the fortune cookie and smoothed the tiny slip of paper. "Says, 'Your initiative will open the way.' "

"Couldn't miss with that one, could they?" Melissa opened hers and read it silently.

"Well?"

"I think there's something un-Christian about reading fortune cookies." She twisted the tiny paper into a wad and tossed it into the wastepaper basket.

"If you decide to live your life following the advice of fortunes, I'd say you were right." But that wasn't what he was thinking. He was thinking how beautiful she looked even with such a hard look on her face. He nibbled a piece of cookie. "Guess it's no sin to eat the cookie?" His grin received no answering smile, only a brisk "No."

She began stacking take-out cartons and clearing the table.

"Hey. What's going on? Melissa, what's wrong?" She had pulled into her shell like a frightened turtle. He wondered whether continuing to probe would bring her out or make her withdraw further.

She gathered up the silverware and took it to the sink. "Nothing."

Her answer was obviously a lie, but he decided not to challenge it. With sudden resolve, he reached for the wastebasket. Something was definitely wrong, and he would get to the bottom of it.

He had the tiny wad in his hand when Melissa turned back toward him. He held it up but couldn't bring himself to open it.

When she spotted the paper, two huge tears rolled down her cheeks.

This went deeper than a fortune cookie. Tyce watched her face crumble. He couldn't stand her misery. A quick step brought him to her, and he gathered her close. Not only her sobbing shook him but the thudding of his heart.

A minute went by, and her tears slowed to an occasional hiccup.

Tyce realized he still clutched the fortune. Gently he smoothed it and read. "A life without love is nothing."

"Will you talk about this?"

She shook her head against his shoulder.

Any moment now she would realize she still stood in his embrace. He hadn't figured out whose love she was weeping over. It surely couldn't be his. The weeping ceased, and Tyce knew she would be terribly embarrassed.

He decided a charge ahead would embarrass her less than a retreat. He slipped the offending fortune paper in his pocket. "I have a couple suggestions that may take the pressure off as far as caring for Darlene is concerned."

As he figured, Melissa straightened and swiped at her eyes.

"One. We are always short-handed at the school. There

must be a number of things Darlene can do. She did just fine helping the volunteers."

"I'm glad to hear that." Melissa reached for a facial tissue from the box on the kitchen counter. "My worst fear was that she'd really mess up."

"The librarian always has books to shelve. I have a whole box of paid invoices needing to be filed. Let's just keep her busy and out of trouble."

Melissa nodded. Tyce couldn't decipher the look on her face. He'd expected a more positive response. He waited.

Finally she met his eyes. "You said that you had a couple suggestions."

"You are not responsible for your mother's illness."

"I know that." Her answer was defensive as he'd expected.

"Knowing it and believing it are two separate things. Intellectually you're aware you didn't cause Darlene to be the way she is. But emotionally you're still carrying all the baggage."

She didn't deny his assessment, but he didn't think she accepted it either. Again he waited, watching her wrestle with the idea. Finally, she picked up the teacups from the table and walked back to the sink. She turned on the water to rinse the cups and silverware before putting them into the dishwasher.

"Perhaps what I feel is guilt that I haven't spent as much time with Mother as I could have." With a dismissive gesture she walked back to face him. "It's too late to fret about what I haven't done. I appreciate your suggestions about keeping Mother busy." She looked at her watch. "I suspect she'll be coming home anytime now." She walked to the hall closet and pulled out his jacket.

The last thing Tyce wanted to do was leave. He didn't think he'd been much help in ridding Melissa of her guilt. Behind her relationship with Darlene lay a lot more than he'd found out. Should he pry?

"What about your father?"

"What about my father?" The words came out almost as a threat.

"You've never spoken about him. I presumed he was dead."

"I presume he is too."

The harsh words stopped Tyce from asking any further questions. He didn't know why she reacted so strongly to the mention of her father, but he'd found the root of Melissa's problem.

The rattle of the key in the door lock stopped him from probing into the matter.

"Mother's home." Her words sounded full of relief. Then a look of panic crossed her face.

"What's wrong?"

"Nothing."

Tyce thought she looked at him like she wished the floor would open up and swallow him. Maybe she didn't want her mother finding him here. "Sorry, there isn't a back door I can sneak out of," he said as Nancy and Darlene entered.

"Good evening, Tyce," Nancy said. "We had a great evening. Darlene and I talked until we almost lost our voices. How's it going, Melissa?"

"Fine."

Nancy turned to Darlene. "We'll have to do this again. I enjoyed your company. Tyce, maybe you can walk me back to my car?"

"Be glad to." He reached for his jacket, which hung from Melissa's limp grasp. "Thanks for the company. See you tomorrow."

"Yes." Then as though coming out of a trance, Melissa added, "The Chinese was delicious. Thank you so much for bringing it. You've both been so thoughtful." She included Nancy in her too bright smile.

Tyce took Nancy's elbow as they stepped out the front door. "Did Darlene do all right?"

"That's the strange thing about dementia. She carried on a

perfectly lucid conversation. She was charming and gracious. Now that she's back with Melissa she may do a complete about-face."

"What do you know about Melissa's dad?"

"Her father? Don't think she's ever mentioned him. Why?"

"I'd like to find out about him."

"He's probably dead, or she would have said something about him."

"Or divorced?"

"Maybe." They reached Nancy's car and she turned to him. "Why this sudden interest in her father?"

"Just something Melissa said tonight. If I'm going to help her, I need to know what's wrong."

"Having a mother with dementia isn't enough?"

"I have a feeling there's a lot more to it than that."

"And you do want to help her?"

Tyce nodded. "I really want to help her."

&

Filing turned out to be something Darlene did well. By noon on Friday, she had Tyce's to-file box cleared out. She'd work for ten to fifteen minutes then sit and rest or shuffle down the hall to Melissa's office. The shuffle-thump, shuffle-thump of Darlene Wilabee became a standard feature around the academic offices.

Melissa looked back on the first week of Darlene's visit. Although it started out with one disaster after another, she felt confident about their working schedule. She could be here in her office and know Darlene was safe and happy.

Melissa smiled, not seeing the papers strewn on the desk in front of her. "Thank you, Lord," she whispered. "Thank you for peace of mind."

Tyce had dropped into her office each morning with a cheery hello. At noon, he brought his lunch over and sat with her and Darlene. He gave no indication that anything unusual had happened between them.

Melissa gradually relaxed as she realized Tyce wasn't going to confront her. Evidently, he'd decided not to pursue the subject of her father. *He's not said one personal thing since Wednesday night.* "Good," she mumbled and felt truly depressed.

"Surprise, surprise."

Startled, Melissa looked up from her desk into Gilbert's grinning face. "What are you doing here?"

Gilbert didn't seem to notice the less than enthusiastic greeting. His laugh echoed down the hallway. "Surprised you, didn't I?"

"You sure did."

"Thought I'd come up and see how Darlene's getting along."

"That's a long trip to check up on Darlene."

Gilbert grinned. "I don't mind. I stopped by the apartment but nobody answered. Where is Darlene?"

"I believe she's in Tyce's office. Right this way." Gilbert trailed behind Melissa. She couldn't help thinking of an obedient puppy. The urge to command "heel" brought a smirk to her lips. "Here we are." She shoved open the door.

"Mother, you have company."

Darlene looked up from the paper she was studying when Melissa stepped aside motioning Gilbert to come in.

"Surprise, surprise."

When Darlene gave him a blank stare, his smile froze in place. Melissa felt sorry for him. She hadn't been exactly welcoming. Tyce must have felt the unease also because he jumped in with, "Hi, Gilbert. Good to see you again."

The mention of Gilbert's name brought a light of recognition to Darlene's face. "Oh, Melissa's boyfriend's back."

Melissa didn't know whose face grew redder, hers or Gilbert's. His face looked pleased and pink. She could only guess what shade hers resembled. But she knew the word pleased would not describe it.

"I have to get back to my office. See you all later." Melissa retreated swiftly.

Neither Darlene nor Gilbert showed up in her office again until quarter to four. Their absence should have made it easier to concentrate on work, but Melissa found her thoughts wandering.

At times she became aware of a tingling sensation around her waist. The memory of Tyce's arms encircling her wiped out all other thoughts. *Don't be a fool, Melissa. No man's worth going through that pain again.*

The noise of someone entering her office brought Melissa out of her reverie.

"What's for dinner?" Gilbert's chortle followed his question. He stepped aside and let Darlene precede him into the room.

"I've invited the boys for dinner."

Melissa didn't ask who the boys were. If she guessed wrong, let it be a pleasant surprise. Then it dawned on her that boys could mean more than two. "So how many are we expecting?"

Darlene's questioning eyebrows made Melissa rephrase her question. No need trying to be subtle. "Who all's coming?"

Gilbert spoke up. "Far as I know, it's Tyce and me." His face took on a troubled look. "You didn't know Darlene was inviting us, did you?"

He looked so contrite, Melissa hastened to reassure him. "My house is Darlene's for this month. She may invite any friends she chooses."

When she switched her gaze to Darlene, she found a pleased expression. "Shall I order us some pizza?" Melissa asked.

"These boys need something besides junk food. How about a nice fried chicken dinner? Mashed potatoes, gravy, green beans, tossed salad. For dessert we should have. . ."

"How about apple pie a la mode?" Gilbert suggested, getting into the spirit of Darlene's feast.

"Perfect." Darlene beamed at Gilbert. "And condiments. Always like olives, pickles, and cranberry sauce with a good meal. Shall we eat about six?"

Six! No way can I make a chicken dinner by then. She hoped her panic didn't show on her face.

"Excuse me." Tyce stood just behind Gilbert in the doorway. "Don't mean to interrupt, but I wondered what time I should arrive for dinner."

Next week might be good. The thought of coming up with a full-fledged holiday type meal by six made Melissa smile. It was too ridiculous to be believed.

Gilbert jumped into the pause after Tyce's question. "About six, Darlene says. We were just deciding on a menu."

Tyce raised skeptical eyebrows. "Obviously this is a spur-of-the-moment plan. What are we having?"

Gilbert gave him a description of the full course.

"Are you a wizard?" Tyce asked Darlene. "That menu would take most people all day."

She seemed to consider his remark for several seconds. "Melissa's in charge."

Valiantly, Melissa kept a straight face.

"Well, when I'm invited out, I don't like to arrive empty-handed. Isn't that right, Gilbert?"

With only a moment's hesitation Gilbert agreed.

"So let's you and I pick up the pie and ice cream. Oh, and one of those rotisserie chickens all the grocery stores have now."

Gilbert nodded to Tyce's suggestion.

"Anything else you need to complete the menu?" His smiling eyes teased a bit. He was having entirely too much fun coming to her rescue.

"I'll manage."

❧

Since Darlene began coming to work with Melissa, each day Melissa had driven the couple of blocks instead of making Darlene walk. Now they reached the car, and Melissa unlocked the door.

"I need to go to the market for a few things. Would you like to come along? Or would you rather I took you back to the apartment first?"

"I think I'd rather go to the apartment. It's been a long day. I'm a little tired."

"Yes, and we have a dozen things to do before the boys arrive."

Once inside the apartment, Melissa checked her cupboards. She set the can of olives out on the counter, found two cans of French sliced green beans, and tossed six large potatoes into the sink. She grabbed a notepad and wrote out the menu.

A few minutes later, with Darlene safely inside the apartment, Melissa sped off to pick up a package of dressing and a can of cranberry sauce. She ran over the list again. A package of brown gravy mix and fresh salad greens completed her shopping. She headed for the checkout counter. A few feet from the line she remembered she had only a tablespoon or two of salad dressing left, so she rushed back to get some. There was bound to be something else she was forgetting, but this would have to do.

At the apartment, she cradled the sack of groceries in one arm and reached for the keys with the other. Inside she checked the clock, quarter to five. Enough time remained to put the potatoes on to boil and then slip into the shower if she hurried. Mother could wash the greens and set the table.

"I'm home, Mother."

Silence.

A prickle of apprehension ran through Melissa. "Mother?" She crossed to the bedroom door and pushed it open. Darlene lay with a blanket over her, shoes neatly lined up beside the bed. Her soft breathing gave testimony to a peaceful sleep.

eight

Relief, then anger, washed over Melissa. Some help Darlene was going to be. She could forget about time to shower. With resolute steps, Melissa headed to the kitchen.

"You're being childish," she admonished herself. "Only three more weeks. You can do this. First, the potatoes."

"Not now. Not now." Petey ruffled his feathers and hopped onto his swing.

"Yes, now," Melissa said. "Good grief. I'm talking back to the bird."

By ten to six the table was set and the aroma of stuffing filled the apartment. Melissa stood back and surveyed the room. She nodded with approval and headed to the bathroom. The least she could do was comb her hair and slip into a clean blouse.

Giving a last pat to her hair, she walked toward the bedroom. Darlene still slept, but her company would be here any minute, and Melissa wasn't about to face the two alone.

"Mother." She gently stroked Darlene's shoulder. "Mother. Time to wake up. Gilbert and Tyce will be here any minute."

Darlene stirred then opened her eyes.

"Company's coming."

Darlene appeared refreshed from her nap. "Where are my shoes?" she asked, sitting up on the edge of the bed.

"Right here." Melissa knelt to guide Darlene's foot into a shoe. "The boys should be here in about two minutes."

The buzzer sounded before Melissa could get back to her feet. "That will be them. You head to the bathroom. I'll get the door."

"Come in. Mother will be out soon."

Gilbert and Tyce entered, each carrying a grocery sack.

"Smells good in here," Gilbert said.

"Make yourselves at home." Melissa took the sack Gilbert held and reached for Tyce's. "Thank you both for bringing this. You get invited to dinner and then end up providing most of it yourselves."

Tyce held on to his bag. "We really came for the company. I'll set this in the kitchen." He followed her as she headed that way.

"Hi, Petey," Gilbert said, putting his finger into the birdcage. "Does Petey come out of his cage and sit on your finger?" he called to Melissa.

"He used to. I guess he still would. I haven't done it since he came."

"Okay if I try?"

"Sure, go ahead."

Melissa could hear Gilbert talking to the bird as she slipped the pie and ice cream out of the sack.

"The chicken will stay hot enough in this carton until we're ready to eat," Tyce said, placing the bag on the counter.

Melissa had just put the ice cream in the freezer when a piercing cry came from the other room. "What are you doing to Petey?" The shouted question came from Darlene.

Melissa rushed to see what was happening. Darlene stood just outside the bathroom door yelling for Gilbert to put Petey back in his cage. Her hair was sopping wet.

Petey took the disturbance as an opportunity to fly from Gilbert's hand to the light fixture hanging over the table. From there he squawked incessantly, adding to the confusion.

"He's trying to steal Petey!" The anguished cry rose from Darlene's throat. Melissa stood transfixed. The whole scene was just too unbelievable. Gilbert was calling and reaching for Petey. Petey climbed to the highest point he could reach, yelling, "Not now. Not now."

Darlene covered her face with her hands, and her wet hair

dripped onto the carpet.

It was Tyce who brought order out of the chaos. "Melissa, why don't you help your mother? Gilbert, the bird will come down by itself when it's ready."

"You think so?"

Tyce's directions put Melissa into action. She put an arm around Darlene and led her toward the bedroom. Passing the bathroom, she reached in and grabbed a towel.

"Don't let him take Petey."

"No, Mother. Petey will stay right here."

"Someone's always trying to take things away from me. But I won't let them. I didn't let them take you, did I?"

"No, Mother."

Melissa settled Darlene into a chair and dried her hair. She realized the blouse was too wet to wear, so she hunted in the closet for a dry one. All the while she fought a feeling of panic. Mother had finally gone over the edge. She couldn't take her back to the college. What if she had a spell in front of everyone? A spell! What a strange word for what she'd just witnessed. A berserk maybe. A paranoia for sure. Why would Darlene think Gilbert was stealing Petey?

Maybe she needed to take Darlene to see a doctor.

By the time Darlene was presentable again, she seemed completely calm.

"Shall we go have dinner now?"

"Yes, I feel quite hungry."

Somehow the guys had restored Petey to his cage. Gilbert sat on the sofa popping his knuckles and looking anywhere but at Darlene and Melissa as they came into the room. Melissa could hear Tyce puttering in the kitchen. The awkward silence stretched until Melissa thought she'd scream.

"Everybody ready to eat?" Tyce called.

"Yeah." Gilbert rose from the sofa and headed toward the kitchen.

"Here, Mother, sit down. I'll see if I can help bring out the food." Unconsciously she straightened her shoulders and followed Gilbert.

"Watch the pan," Tyce said as Gilbert reached to pick up the stuffing. "I put it in the oven to stay warm."

Melissa glanced at her watch; it was twenty to seven. It had taken her longer than she thought to get Darlene calm and presentable.

Thanks to Tyce, all the food was hot. Melissa managed to down a few bites, but her appetite was gone. Darlene hadn't spoken since she sat down at the table. Melissa couldn't decide if Darlene was embarrassed by her outburst or didn't even remember what had happened.

Even Tyce was having trouble keeping the conversation rolling. He asked Gilbert about his trip from Turner to Seattle, covered work-related incidents, and commented on the weather.

Melissa shoved another forkful of potatoes around her plate. Tyce and Gilbert had cleaned their plates, and Darlene's was almost empty.

"Are we ready for dessert?" Melissa picked up her plate as she shoved back from the table.

"Let me help," Tyce said.

"That's all right. I can get it." Melissa needed a few minutes to herself, although the kitchen didn't provide her with much privacy. She'd just pulled the ice cream out of the freezer when the phone rang.

"Hello."

"Hi, Melissa. This is Beverly. We don't have a very good connection. How's it going?"

Should she really tell her? Maybe not in front of the audience, who had all grown quiet as she picked up the phone. "We'll manage. How's your trip?"

"Marvelous. We have really good news. Charles received a special bonus for the work he's doing here."

"That's great. Mother will be pleased."

"Can I talk to Mom?"

"Sure. Just a minute." Melissa took the cordless phone to Darlene. "It's Beverly. She's calling to let us know Charles received a bonus. Here, she'll tell you about it."

Darlene took the phone. "Hello."

Darlene's side of the conversation wasn't very enlightening. She responded to Beverly with nods and an occasional "yes." "I'll tell her," she said and handed the phone back to Melissa.

"Beverly?" Melissa pushed the phone closer to her ear. "Hello?"

"She already hung up," Darlene informed her.

"I wanted to ask her a couple things." Melissa frowned at the phone. "You said, 'I'll tell her.' Did Beverly have a message for me?"

Darlene nodded then popped the last bit of chicken on her plate into her mouth.

Melissa waited while Darlene chewed. Tyce and Gilbert waited in silence for Darlene to repeat the message. Finally, Melissa couldn't stand it. "What did she say?"

The blank look on Darlene's face gave Melissa the horrible feeling that Darlene wasn't going to remember the message.

"It was about Charles's bonus," Darlene said. "Were you getting us pie and ice cream?"

"Yes. It will be coming right up. But what did Beverly say about the bonus?"

"He gets an extra three weeks' vacation."

"Wow!" Gilbert exclaimed. "Three weeks. That's quite a bonus."

Tyce nodded.

Melissa walked back into the kitchen. She picked up the knife to cut the pie. Something didn't sound right. Beverly wasn't one for keeping in touch unless she wanted something from you. But the vacation was pretty significant news.

Pulling the dessert plates out of the cupboard, an idea crossed her mind. "Did Beverly say when they were taking vacation?"

"No."

Melissa scooped ice cream onto the first piece of pie.

"She did say it was a great opportunity to see Europe as long as they were over there."

The scoop hovered over the ice cream carton. "I knew it!" She wanted to scream, to kick something, to throw herself on the bed and cry. The bed. She wouldn't sleep in her own bed for another six weeks.

⁂

Tyce came to the same conclusion Melissa did, and he watched her face as the realization swept over her. The struggle was written in the droop of her mouth and the widening of her eyes. If the phone call had come before Darlene's outburst, it would have been easier to take.

He rose and picked up both his and Gilbert's dirty plates. He wanted to comfort Melissa, but what could he say or do with Darlene and Gilbert watching?

After setting the dishes in the sink, Tyce took the ice cream scoop from Melissa's hand and dipped ice cream onto the remaining pieces of pie. "You carry these two. I'll get these," he said, holding two plates toward Melissa.

She seemed to be working on autopilot now. Her facial expression was blank. Taking the plates, she walked to the table. They ate their dessert in silence.

Her misery is killing me. But what can I do? First he needed to find out more about Darlene's condition. Ignorance wasn't bliss in this case. Melissa needed help in understanding what was going on.

And secondly, he had to break the pall settling over them.

"Well, Gilbert, what are your plans for the weekend?" Tyce forced as much cheer into his question as he could.

"I. . .I'm not exactly sure." Gilbert's glance bounced off Melissa and Darlene and came back to Tyce.

"Let's see. We could drive up to Edmonds and catch a ferry over to Kingston. There is a good little restaurant there." Whatever was going to happen this weekend, Tyce was counting himself in. If Melissa didn't want him coming along, she could tell him so. Until Gilbert showed some initiative, he'd take charge.

"Hey, it's getting late. I'll bet you're tired after all the work you did for me in my office." Tyce smiled at Darlene. "What time shall I pick you up for the ferry ride?"

"That sounds like fun. If we're going to have lunch there, I guess we need to leave early. How long is the ride?" Darlene's eyes lit up at the idea, and her old animation came back.

"It'll take us twenty minutes to drive to the ferry dock. Don't know how long the wait will be. Sometimes there's quite a backup on weekends. The actual ferry ride is less than half an hour."

Tyce looked to Melissa for confirmation. "Okay if we meet here at ten?"

She nodded.

"Come on, Gilbert, we need to let these ladies get their beauty sleep. Not that you aren't already beautiful," he added hastily.

Darlene beamed. "Melissa, why haven't you married this man? He certainly knows how to make a girl feel good."

Before Melissa could say anything, Tyce jumped in. "Now, Darlene, don't let a few flattering words go to your head. After all, you're my date for tomorrow, and I'll think you're trying to get rid of me if you go shoving me off on Melissa. Besides, Gilbert here might take offense." He gave Gilbert a playful tap on the arm.

Everyone was smiling except Melissa. Her stony face gave no indication of what she thought.

"Thank you for inviting us over," Tyce said shaking Darlene's hand. Then he turned his back on Gilbert and Darlene and reached for Melissa's hand. He held it gently between both of his. For long seconds their eyes locked. There was so much he wanted to tell her.

"Not now. Not now," Petey yelled.

nine

Tyce walked with Gilbert to his car. "Melissa's having a really hard time dealing with her mom's condition. We need to do what we can to help her out."

"She really spooked me out about Petey. Why would she think I was trying to steal him?"

"Dementia does strange things to the mind. You'll have to remember this isn't the same Darlene you knew as a kid. The disease has changed her."

"Guess I didn't realize it was so bad. How does Melissa cope?"

"Right now she's not doing very well. And you did understand that Beverly's not coming back for six weeks instead of three, didn't you?"

Gilbert nodded. "Do you think my coming up here makes it worse?"

"I can't answer that. You'll have to ask Melissa. Anyway, tomorrow let's both do all we can to help Melissa get through this."

"Right." Gilbert's response sounded doubtful.

Tyce walked across the courtyard to his own apartment. He needed to find information on dementia. He headed toward the computer and accessed the Web. A couple of hours later, he'd printed off two dozen pages describing the effects of the disease and how it eroded a person's ability to reason. He'd read case histories and looked up resources for helping caregivers.

What he'd discovered didn't give him much hope. The task of caring for Darlene was only going to get harder.

❧

Melissa rolled and tossed on the sofa bed. What was she to do with Mother? She went over and over the scene. Darlene hadn't given a reason for trying to wash her hair. Finally, she sat up and threw her robe around her shoulders. *Is Mother going crazy? Why was she screaming at Gilbert?*

Nothing made sense. The more she thought about the evening, the tighter the tension grew in the back of her neck. She could tell a roaring headache would result from what she now called "the nightmare." Only she'd been wide awake.

Melissa drew the robe closer and paced the floor. Six more weeks! But Beverly's return would not take care of the problem of Mother's health.

The decision to take some aspirin tablets for her pounding head came just as a noise emerged from the bedroom. She heard the distinct squeak of the closet door opening. Was Mother up moving around, or had someone broken in through the bedroom window?

Melissa held her breath waiting for another sound from the bedroom. Her palms grew sweaty as indecision kept her rooted to the carpet. What if Mother were in trouble? When no further noises came from the room, she decided her imagination had gotten the better of her.

"I found him. He's hiding under the bed." Darlene burst out of the bedroom dressed in the blue skirt from earlier in the day, topped by a brown blouse, and her stockingless feet were shoved into black shoes. The blouse, buttoned incorrectly, hung lopsided on her frame.

Melissa grabbed Darlene and backed away from the bedroom until she could reach the phone. She punched in 911 and realized she could hardly do it because she was shaking so badly.

"911. What is your emergency?"

"Someone has broken into my apartment." Her voice came out in a scratchy whisper.

"Are they armed?"

"I don't know. Mother, did you see who broke in? Did they have a gun?"

Darlene stared at Melissa with uncomprehending eyes.

"Mother!" Melissa gave her a little shake. "Did you see who came in the window?"

"Is that how the cat got in?"

"Cat?"

"Yes. I cornered him under the bed."

"Ma'am. Do you still need emergency assistance?" the 911 operator asked.

"I'm sorry. There seems to be some confusion. Sorry to have bothered you."

Grinning like a child with a secret, Darlene motioned for Melissa to follow her into the bedroom. "It's under there."

Melissa looked at the window, then walked closer and jiggled the latch. "The window's locked."

"Look. Look under there." Darlene grabbed Melissa's arm, pulling her toward the bed.

Melissa got on her knees and peered under the bed. Realizing the room was too dark to see anything, she crossed to the switch and flicked on the light. Then she opened the nightstand drawer and pulled out the flashlight she kept there. Once again on her knees, she directed the light into each corner.

"There isn't anything under here."

"Aha! He got away again."

Melissa rocked back on her heels and stared at her mother. There never had been anyone or anything in the bedroom. It was all in Darlene's mind.

"Why are you dressed? It's the middle of the night."

As though addressing an ignorant child, Darlene said, "You can't chase a cat in your nightgown."

The absurdity of the answer struck Melissa's funny bone. She laughed until the tears rolled down her face. Then the laughter turned to anguish and the tears continued to fall.

❧

When the alarm went off at seven A.M., Melissa rolled over

and groaned. She'd finally fallen asleep about four. Or at least that was the last time she remembered looking at the clock. After getting Darlene back into her nightgown and into bed, there'd been no further noise from the bedroom.

Now Melissa wondered why she ever agreed to the ferry ride. The last thing she wanted was to keep up appearances before Tyce and Gilbert. Reluctantly, she threw back the covers and headed to the bathroom.

Feeling refreshed from the quick shower, she curled up in the overstuffed chair with her Bible. The bookmark directed her to the Psalms. She read Psalm 121.

> I lift up my eyes to the hills—
> > where does my help come from?
> My help comes from the Lord,
> > the Maker of heaven and earth.
> He will not let your foot slip—
> > he who watches over you will not slumber;
> indeed, he who watches over Israel
> > will neither slumber nor sleep.

"Lord, you and I must have been up together most of the night." Melissa smiled at the thought. Then she realized how little awareness there had been on her part. She'd fretted, worried, rebelled. And all the time she could have been seeking God. Seeking the God who watched over her day and night.

"Lord, You know my needs. You know Mother's needs. You understand her even if I don't." *Mother's needs!* The light bulb of understanding flashed through Melissa's consciousness. "Forgive me, Lord. I've only thought about my own needs. I've considered how my routine is upset, how my apartment is in disarray, and what people will think of me when Mother behaves strangely. What does she need?"

The shuffle-thump, shuffle-thump announced Darlene as she emerged from the bedroom in her nightgown.

"Good morning, Mother."

Darlene looked up but made no reply. She headed into the bathroom. When she still hadn't come out again after thirty-five minutes, Melissa tapped lightly on the door. "Everything all right in there?"

Darlene didn't answer.

"Are you okay?" This time Melissa didn't wait for an answer. She eased open the door. Darlene had a nearly empty shampoo bottle in her hand. The contents of the bottle oozed from her hair and dripped onto the shoulders of her nightgown. Towels draped over the sink and stool and lay bunched on the floor.

For a moment, Melissa could only stare. Every clean towel in the bathroom was covered with sticky shampoo.

"I can't get it off." Darlene's plaintive voice snapped Melissa into action. She helped Darlene out of the sticky nightgown and into the shower, where buckets of shampoo suds went down the drain.

"I'll be right back," she called. Hurrying to the kitchen, she snatched up hand towels and raced back to the bath. She picked up all the sticky towels and tossed them into the hamper. It could be worse. After all, the mess was just soap.

Darlene submitted to Melissa's care as she dried her off and led her to the bedroom. Melissa opened the closet and glanced through the clothes. What should Darlene wear? Something warm. The ferry ride would be cold this time of year.

❧

The morning overcast burnt off, and the October day turned sunny. Seagulls flew over the whipped cream wake of the ferry, and the Olympic Mountains stood majestically over Puget Sound. Melissa looked at all the beauty surrounding her, trying to soak in the reassurance of its Creator. He was in charge of mountains and oceans. He could surely take care of her and Darlene.

Tyce and Gilbert had arrived in good spirits. Gilbert, grinning like Alice's Cheshire cat, had handed each lady a box of chocolates.

"Why, Gilbert, how thoughtful," Darlene said, already tearing off the plastic wrapper. There was no sign of her earlier frustration.

But the switch in Darlene's behavior only made Melissa more insecure. She watched her mother closely. Maybe she could discover some signal indicating a coming spell. She grimaced at the choice of words. The old Darlene would throw a fit if it were suggested she had spells.

"Sorry, I come empty-handed," Tyce said, spreading both hands in front of him.

Darlene patted his arm. "Your presence is enough."

For once, Melissa agreed with her mother. When he walked in the door and smiled at her, the knot of nervous tension in her stomach started unwinding.

"If you ladies are ready?" Tyce offered his arm to Darlene. "Let's get this show on the road."

They'd had only a brief ferry wait at the dock before loading, which they all agreed wasn't bad for a Saturday morning. Once the ferry was under way, they strolled around the boat until Darlene declared she needed to rest and chose a seat by a side window.

"Gilbert, you come keep me company." Darlene patted the seat beside her. Without waiting for comment from anyone, she continued, "Tyce, you take Melissa out front there and watch the scenery."

The three young adults looked at each other. Almost in unison they shrugged their shoulders. As Gilbert sat down next to Darlene, Tyce said, "We won't be gone long."

Melissa couldn't decide whether to laugh or be angry with her mother. She'd always been a manipulator, and it appeared dementia hadn't changed that.

"Shall we?" Tyce swept his hand toward the front of the ferry. "Why not?"

They strolled in silence and rested their arms on the rail when they reached the bow. A sharp wind blew Melissa's hair around her face. She pulled her jacket collar up but shivered despite the sunshine.

"Maybe we better step back behind the windows," Tyce suggested. "No sense getting really cold." They moved behind the panels of glass looking out over the bow of the ferry. "That's better."

Silence stretched between them, but Melissa didn't feel uncomfortable. She relaxed and watched the white caps break over the water. When she stole a glance at Tyce, he was watching her.

"How did it go after we left last night?"

"Fine." The word popped out before Melissa gave it any thought. Then she grinned at Tyce. "Okay, not fine. But we're here." The overpowering urge to tell him the story of the cat episode and the shampoo disaster made Melissa clamp her mouth shut.

"Last night I did some searching on the Web to find out more about dementia."

Melissa froze. To have someone else call it by name made Mother's illness sound so final.

"Don't know whether you've looked into it." Tyce paused.

She knew he was expecting her to respond. All she could do was shake her head.

"Knowing what's happening and what to expect might make it easier."

She nodded unconvinced.

"It's not going to go away or get better."

Melissa wanted to scream at him to be quiet. This was a beautiful day and a wonderful view, and the last thing she wanted to do was spoil it by talking about her mother's problems. Instead, she listened as he described the symptoms.

"This morning she seems perfectly reasonable."

Melissa nodded again while scenes from the previous night

flashed through her mind.

"Tomorrow or next week or in five minutes she may do or say something really outrageous."

"How do you know when it's going to happen?" She suddenly realized she wanted to know. There didn't seem to be anything worse than not knowing.

"You don't. And she doesn't. And a lot of the time she won't be aware she is saying or doing anything unusual."

"But last night she—" Melissa stopped in mid-sentence. She had no intention of telling him about the cat incident.

"The information I read said such delusions are common."

Melissa opened her mouth but nothing came out. He couldn't know about Darlene's behavior.

"Thinking that someone is stealing your property is part of the paranoia."

"Oh, you mean when she thought Gilbert was stealing Petey?"

"That's what I was referring to," Tyce said. "What else did she do last night?"

Melissa stared across the water.

"It might help to talk about it. Just know that I'm ready to listen anytime you want to talk. Okay?" He gave her shoulders a quick squeeze. "We told Gilbert we wouldn't be gone long. Maybe we better get back." Tyce started to turn then pointed to a black object in the water about forty feet from the ferry. "What's that?"

The black disappeared under a white cap and then bobbed back to the surface. "It's a seal." Melissa peered eagerly at the water. "Oh, look. There's another one. We should have brought binoculars."

"Let's go tell Gilbert and Darlene. I bet they'd like to see them."

ten

"Come on over to the other side," Tyce called as he and Melissa neared the plastic padded seats where Gilbert and Darlene sat. "You have to see the seals."

Five small seals bobbed in and out of the water by the time they reached the windows on the far side.

"Wow!" Gilbert shoved his face close to the glass. "You don't see sights like this in Turner."

The animals played to their audience several minutes before disappearing beneath the waves. "Where did they go?" asked a small child who had joined them to enjoy the display.

"I'll bet their mother called them home because it was time for lunch," Gilbert said, grinning at the boy.

A puzzled frown formed on the boy's face. "Do they have a home?"

Gilbert's laugh echoed through the ferry. "You got me there."

The overhead speaker crackled to life. "Will all passengers please return to their cars in preparation for docking. Walk-on passengers will disembark from the upper deck."

"Billy!" The call came from a frazzled-looking woman balancing a baby on her hip. "Billy, get back over here." The boy cast a last look at Gilbert before slowly obeying his mother's summons.

The restaurant at the end of the ferry dock had a view over the water. Melissa watched seagulls collecting on the pier pilings and a couple of ducks searching for tidbits tossed up from the ferry's propeller.

"What looks good?" Tyce asked the group in general. "I usually end up with the same old hamburger and fries."

"This soup and salad combo sounds good," Melissa said. "It's just cool enough out to make hot soup inviting. What would you like, Mother?"

Darlene settled on a Caesar salad and cup of chili. When their orders arrived, Gilbert leaned back in the booth and crossed his arms over his chest. "Guess this is as good a time as any to share my news." He had everyone's attention immediately.

"What news?" Melissa asked.

"I've received an offer from the company to transfer to California."

"But you just moved back to Turner." Melissa stopped with her spoon halfway to her mouth. "Your folks aren't going to be happy about you taking off again so soon."

"No. Suppose not. But it's a opportunity for advancement."

"Why didn't you say something yesterday?" Melissa gave him a teasing look. "You must have been dying to share your news with us."

"I was still thinking on it."

Melissa caught the look on Gilbert's face, and realization dawned. *He thought I might want him to stay closer on my account!* She took a large spoonful of her cream of broccoli soup and promptly burnt her mouth. She sputtered and gulped and took a sip of water.

"You okay?" Darlene asked. "Sure is good chili. Careful though, it's hot. You could burn your mouth."

The absurdity brought a giggle to Melissa's lips. There wasn't anything she could reply to that. She was still sipping water trying to cool her mouth. And what could she say to Gilbert? Nothing he wanted to hear.

What a bunch we are! she thought, scraping up the last shreds of her salad.

Suddenly Darlene looked up from her meal. "When are you coming back to see us, Gilbert?"

"He's heading to California, Mother."

Darlene considered that a moment and then nodded. "That's best. Melissa has chosen Tyce anyway."

If Melissa could have been more embarrassed she couldn't figure how it could be possible. She chased a piece of lettuce around her plate and refused to look up.

"Anyone here care for dessert?" the waitress asked.

Tyce took charge. "I think we're done. Thank you."

The waitress nodded and tore the bill from her pad. "Thank you for coming in."

"I'll take care of that," Gilbert said, reaching for the slip of paper. Tyce didn't argue. Melissa thought she should object but hadn't the courage to look Gilbert in the face.

The ferry ride back was uncomfortable. Everything she thought of to talk about seemed either too trivial or too pointed. She'd like to know more about Gilbert's new job. How did she go about asking?

The problem was solved when Tyce began questioning Gilbert. "Does this move mean a raise or a promotion?"

To Melissa's surprise, Gilbert sounded excited about this new opportunity; with enthusiasm, he described his new position. He and Tyce were soon talking about technology she didn't understand.

&

"Thank you," Darlene said. "That was a really nice day." She climbed out of the car and headed for the apartment. She was looking very independent as she shuffle-thumped her way over the sidewalk.

"Thank you." Melissa looked first Gilbert and then Tyce straight in the eye. "Thank you for the ride and the lunch. And thanks for understanding about Mother." A reality had dawned on her as she sat feeling sorry for herself during the last several minutes. Tyce had been right. Mother wasn't going to get better. So she'd better adjust.

&

A postcard came from Beverly. It pictured the Tower of London and the guards. "Having a marvelous time," Beverly wrote.

Melissa brought the card to Darlene after work. For the last three days, Darlene had accompanied Melissa to work in the mornings, then come back to the apartment for an afternoon nap. Melissa wasn't getting a lot of work done in the afternoons. Her mind kept dwelling on all the things that could go wrong with Darlene being by herself. There had to be a better arrangement, but she hadn't found it.

Darlene read the card. "Humph. Wordy, isn't she."

Melissa laughed out loud. For the moment, Mother was her old self.

"What are we going to do this evening?"

"I didn't have anything planned," Melissa said. "Would you like to go see a movie?"

"I haven't been to a movie in years. What's on?"

Melissa reached for the paper. "Let's see. We have a choice of a presidential assassination, a world war, an alien attack, or a scientific experiment gone awry. Or here's a Hollywood triangle, or maybe that's a quadrangle. Sorry I suggested the movies. I don't see anything worth paying to go see." Melissa waited for her mother to respond.

"I want to go home," Darlene said.

The declaration surprised Melissa. Darlene hadn't said anything about returning to Turner in the two and a half weeks she'd been here. What had brought this sudden desire? "I guess you miss Beverly and the familiar surroundings."

"I miss Beverly and Melissa. They were such cute little girls."

In stunned silence, Melissa watched her mother. Never in all her life had Mother once said she was cute. Had she really thought so? Then how come Melissa had spent her childhood identifying with the Ugly Duckling instead of Cinderella or Snow White?

"I got to keep them both too. Franklin was no match for me."

The mention of her father's name stopped the words trembling on Melissa's lips. What was Mother saying?

"Beverly and I managed. She was such a good little actress.

When that judge asked her if she wanted to live with me, she puckered up and said, 'Not without Melissa.' " A cackle escaped the twisting lips. "That did it. Over Franklin's protests I got you both. I got the house. I got the car." The sneer on Darlene's face turned to bitter hatred.

Melissa held her breath. What else would Mother say?

Darlene sat rocking back and forth in a mesmerizing rhythm. Her hands picked at the hem of her lavender pullover. "There wasn't any proof. I was careful about that. Franklin was so sanctimonious." Darlene spoke in short, choppy sentences that didn't make sense to Melissa. But she listened in absolute silence—not moving—afraid to break the spell.

Finally, Darlene relaxed and looked about her as though seeing the living room for the first time. Her hands quieted in her lap.

Still Melissa said nothing.

"We should play a game of cards." The abrupt switch in subjects caught Melissa still wondering about the past.

"Mother?" Hesitantly she called her mother's attention to her.

"Yes."

"You were talking about Daddy."

"Was I?"

"You said you won custody of me over Daddy's protests."

"Of course I did."

"When I was little, you said Daddy. . ." She swallowed the lump forming in her throat. "You said Daddy left and wanted nothing more to do with us."

With a negligent shrug Darlene eyed her daughter. "You moped around bad enough as it was. If I'd told you about the letters and phone calls, you would have pestered me to death to see your father."

Anger so strong it made her stomach churn overwhelmed Melissa. "Letters! Daddy sent me letters?"

"That was twenty-some years ago. Why are you getting so excited?"

Melissa's mind boggled at the sudden revelation. Twenty-five years! Twenty-five years of hate and anger. Twenty-five years of lost relationship. Twenty-five years of believing lies.

She had a father somewhere who loved her enough to fight for custody, send her letters, call her on the phone. . . . "Do you still have my letters?"

Darlene looked past Melissa to where Petey had taken up his refrain. "Not now. Not now." Her brows furrowed over blank eyes.

"Mother," Melissa almost shouted. "Don't you go weird on me now. I want to know what you did with my letters."

"I don't remember."

"Did you burn them?"

Darlene shook her head.

"Did you keep them?"

"Yes."

"Where?"

"I don't remember." Darlene's face crumbled in hopelessness. "I really don't remember. You hate me, don't you?"

Yes! Of all the emotions Melissa had ever felt, nothing seemed as horrible as the roiling tempest within her. She stood and took a step toward her bedroom; Mother had taken that too.

"I'm going out." She grabbed a jacket and her keys. The door slammed softly behind her. At the car, she changed her mind about driving and stuffed the keys into her pocket. The sun hid behind gray clouds. A strong northwesterly wind blew them at a brisk pace. Melissa pulled the jacket on and zipped it to her chin. Long strides took her away from the apartment. Her arms pumped in a rhythm bent on covering as much ground as possible.

Two miles later she slowed her pace. Streetlights made little pools of light in the evening darkness. *What am I to do, Lord? What am I to do?* Unconsciously, the prayer had tumbled over and over in her mind. Now it came to the surface.

She spoke into the empty street.

"What do You want me to do?"

A drop of rain landed on her cheek, followed closely by another, then another. They ran down her face like tears.

Melissa pushed on until she was exhausted then headed back. Her mind was no more settled when she reached the apartment block than when she'd left. The light sprinkle had turned to a steady drizzle, matting her hair to her head and soaking through the shoulders of her jacket.

I'll probably catch a cold. The possibility seemed unimportant. Nothing seemed important. Her mind resembled the gray Seattle weather. All the edges were blurred. Fatigue dulled her senses. She just wanted to curl up in her own bed, cradle her Snoopy dog, and forget.

The hall light picked up the white glare of a piece of paper stuck to the apartment door.

> *Darlene's at my apartment.*
> *Come over or call when you get back.*
> > *Tyce*

Melissa read it twice.

"Mother?" Melissa called as she opened the door. She truly hoped the note was wrong. What was Mother doing at Tyce's apartment? Couldn't she stay put for the short time Melissa had been gone?

"Not now."

Melissa grabbed the cover and flung it over Petey's cage. She almost smiled. Those were her sentiments exactly. Mother couldn't be at Tyce's. Not now.

&

Tyce answered on the first ring. "Hello."

"This is Melissa. Is Darlene there?"

"Sure is. Are you ready to have me escort her home?" There was a brief hesitation before he heard Melissa's voice.

"Yes. Thank you."

Tyce hung up and turned to Darlene. "It's gotten cool out. Let me get you a sweater before I walk you back to the apartment." He draped an oversized cable cardigan around her shoulders.

Seeing how it hung on Darlene he said, "Now I do feel like an elephant."

"It's nice having a big man around. It gives a girl a feeling of security."

Tyce chuckled as Darlene slid an arm into a sleeve and waved the four-inch extension of knit fabric at him. He tried to push the sleeve up her arm, but it promptly slid back down. "Oh, well. Guess we're not trying to make a fashion statement."

From Tyce's end of the apartment complex to Melissa's was about half a block. At Darlene's pace it took ten minutes to reach the door. She clung to his arm for support.

"We're here," Tyce announced unnecessarily as Melissa opened the door. She stepped back making room for them to enter without comment.

Darlene's hand tightened on his arm. She seemed uncertain, hesitant to enter. He reassured her with a gentle pat. "You've had quite an evening. Do you want to go lie down?"

She nodded.

Tyce could feel the tension between the two women. He couldn't figure out what had gone on. Darlene's explanation didn't quite tell the whole story. But it was for sure he wasn't going to leave them alone just yet.

"There's your cane. You can't go out for a walk again without that." He handed it to her.

Without saying a word to Melissa, Darlene headed toward the bedroom. And Melissa watched her go just as quietly.

"I found her wandering in the complex." He decided it was up to him to break the silence. "We came back to the apartment, but she didn't have her key so I just took her home."

"Thank you. That was very kind."

"Whoa! I know something big must have happened here tonight. But why do I get the feeling I'm being treated like an outsider?" He watched the emotions contort Melissa's face.

"Look, I'm not leaving until I know you're all right."

"All right? I don't think I will ever be all right."

Tyce glanced toward the bedroom. "Do you need to check and see if Darlene's in bed?"

"So far she's been quite able to put herself to bed."

"Are you going to tell me what happened?" In two steps he was beside her and had an arm securely around her shoulders. "I can tell you're not going to get any rest tonight if you don't take the cork out of this bottle. You look ready to explode."

Melissa nodded but remained silent.

"Darlene said you just got mad and stomped out, and she was worried about you."

"That's all she said?"

"That's it."

"Guess she was right. I did stomp out. It was that or, like you say, explode."

"Did she break something, try and wash her hair again, think someone was stealing Petey?"

"Oh, this had nothing to do with her dementia. She did this when she was in complete control of her faculties."

Tyce nudged Melissa toward the sofa. "Could we sit?" She'd relaxed under the pressure of his arm. He could feel her shoulders sag. He was tempted to fire a dozen questions at her, but he held his tongue. She needed to tell him in her own way, her own time. At least he hoped she'd tell him. Whatever it was, it had to be bad.

The minute of silence stretched into two.

"Lord, we know You are in charge of Your universe. But sometimes we just don't understand why things are the way they are." Tyce paused, waiting for the Spirit to guide him. He had an audience of two. God would understand what his heart was trying to say even if he faltered in getting the words right.

This prayer was for Melissa; he had to get it right for her.

"Melissa is struggling with the past, Lord. We know Your Word says to forget the past and press on. To forgive those who trespass against us. We try, Lord, but it's not easy.

"So for my friend Melissa I ask for a double measure of peace in dealing with the unpeaceful, love to give the unlovely, patience for handling frustrations, self-control when she just wants to scream, and goodness and kindness for those times when caring for Darlene seems overwhelming. Amen."

eleven

There were no sounds coming from the bedroom. It seemed Mother had gotten herself to bed. At least she wasn't chasing imaginary cats around the room.

Tyce had concluded his prayer, and Melissa supposed she should say something. She'd closed her mind to everything except the comforting feel of his arm around her shoulder. If she spoke, the spell would be broken. The words of his prayer crept into her thoughts. Love, patience, self-control.

"If I'm to have the fruit of the Spirit, what happened to joy?" The bitter sound of her voice surprised even her. And to her amazement he chuckled.

"I wondered if you'd notice."

"So you left out joy on purpose?"

"Not exactly on purpose as you mean it. Joy comes from doing what God wants us to. I have a feeling you're not quite ready to open up to joy. You have a few things to work through first."

"How did you get so smart?"

"Maybe by working my way to joy a couple of times. Are you ready to tell me about Darlene?"

She sighed, not sure where to begin. "Somewhere I have a father who loves me."

"Isn't that good?"

"Yeah, it would be except I grew up thinking he hated me." She looked into Tyce's face and saw the puzzlement. "Aren't you going to ask why?"

"Why?" he finally said.

"Because my mother lied to me and told me he wanted nothing more to do with us."

88

"Now that you know the truth, what are you going to do about it?" He took his arm from her shoulder and sat forward. Resting his elbows on his knees, he tented his fingers and rested them against his pursed lips. "Do you know where he lives?"

Melissa shook her head.

"Does your mom know?"

"I don't think so." Her mind wandered to twenty-five years in the past. A little five-year-old holding a willow branch fishing pole and looking up at a smiling father. "He did love me."

"I think I detected a little joy in those words. Think you'll be all right for the night? You need some rest."

"I'll be all right." To her surprise she believed it.

৵

Thursday morning Melissa awoke to the sound of running water. "Oh, no!" She threw her robe on and headed to the bathroom. The door was ajar, and she pushed it open. Neatly folded on the counter was Darlene's nightgown. The bath mat lay on the floor, and from behind the curtain came the sound of splashing water.

With a conscious effort Melissa relaxed, letting her shoulders sag. This morning, anyway, Darlene was taking a normal shower.

Melissa had pulled a couple of bowls from the cupboard before her thoughts returned to the night before. Her mind replayed Tyce's question. "What are you going to do about it?"

What was there to do? She couldn't relive the last twenty-five years. Hatred was an ugly thing. It crept in and nested below the subconscious. All these years the hatred would pop up when least expected. She'd see a happy family laughing together, and the hatred would rear its ugly head. The force of that emotion exploded into such bitterness toward her father she'd be physically sick to her stomach.

And Dad wasn't to blame.

Somewhere in the last few days she remembered reading about bitterness. It was a pamphlet that crossed her desk at school. What had it said?

Her Bible concordance rested on the bookcase beside the TV. She thumbed through the pages until she reached BIT. Glancing down the list of references she found what she was looking for.

With Bible in hand, she curled up in the corner of the sofa. Opening her Bible, she turned to Hebrews chapter twelve. There, in verses fourteen and fifteen, she read:

"Make every effort to live in peace with all men and to be holy; without holiness no one will see the Lord. See to it that no one misses the grace of God and that no bitter root grows up to cause trouble. . . ."

She read the verses over and over. *No bitter root. Well, thanks to Mother I have a huge root that will take a stump puller to get rid of. How do I dispel years of bitterness toward my father?*

As she thought the word *father,* she paused for the pain. It didn't happen. Knowledge had wiped out hatred in a single twelve-hour period.

"Of all the wasted emotional energy!"

"Did you say something?" Darlene entered the room fully dressed, her hair combed and makeup in place.

Melissa turned and discovered the missing anger; in full force it had been transferred to Darlene. She gripped the Bible with both hands. *Make every effort. Make every effort.* Like a mantra, she repeated it over and over in her mind.

"Good morning." Melissa smiled. The anger abated. "You're looking nice."

"Thank you."

❧

Thursday morning slid by with a heavy workload. By eleven-thirty, Melissa could see a bare spot on her desk and a neat stack of forms filled out for the next term. Keeping on top of the mountain of paper for government student loans demanded constant diligence. She pushed back with a sense of accomplishment. She should probably check on Darlene. She'd left her filing in the business office a few hours ago. With her thoughts back on Darlene, Tyce's question returned. *What are you going to do about it?*

Suddenly the plan seemed clear. She would find her father. Maybe Mother knew some way to get in touch with him. If not, there were a number of ways to track people down. And the letters. There was an upstairs bedroom in the house at Turner full of Darlene's stored possessions. If Darlene kept Melissa's letters from her father, they would be up there.

She could go to Turner this weekend. If she left right after work, she might be there in five hours. That would depend on five o'clock traffic out of Seattle. As Melissa walked down the hall, she mulled over the idea. She'd pack a suitcase tonight. When would be the best time to tell Darlene they were going? Probably tonight.

Melissa opened the business office door and halted in midstride. Papers littered the floor. Darlene stood at the filing cabinet. "I can't find it," she complained.

Melissa rushed forward and caught Darlene's arm before the next folder joined the disaster on the floor. "What can't you find?"

Darlene jerked her arm trying to break free from Melissa's hold. She wagged her head back and forth. "I can't find it."

"What in the world happened here?"

Melissa spun around to find Tyce standing in the doorway. She momentarily lost her grip on Darlene, and another folder hit the floor.

Before Melissa could speak, Tyce was across the room gently enfolding Darlene in his large embrace. "Come on." He urged her away from the cabinet.

She resisted, then let him lead her to the chair behind the desk.

Melissa stooped to retrieve a file.

"Leave it for now," Tyce said. "Come on, Darlene, I think you've had enough work for one day. Let's get you back to the apartment." Melissa took one arm and Tyce the other as they walked Darlene out to the car. She had stopped grumbling about not finding "it," whatever "it" was. Melissa couldn't blot out the image of Tyce's office. It would take hours to restore the files.

Melissa unlocked the apartment and stepped back to let Darlene and Tyce enter.

"You've had a busy morning." Tyce helped Darlene remove her coat. "Maybe you should go rest for a few minutes."

Darlene nodded and headed toward the bedroom.

"I'm so sorry." Melissa could feel tears threatening to fall.

"I know." Tyce reached for her hands. "No permanent damage has been done. It can all be put back." He squeezed her fingers. "And if anyone is to blame, I am. I should have known not to leave Darlene alone."

"What was she looking for?"

To Melissa's surprise Tyce chuckled. "She probably won't even remember she messed up the files, let alone what she was looking for."

"Obviously she can't be trusted to do filing anymore."

"Not in my office."

Melissa caught the wink, and they laughed together.

"How can you be such a good sport about this? When I saw that mess, I wanted to scream."

"For one thing, she's not my mother."

"What does that mean?"

"Haven't you noticed? It's a lot easier to be sympathetic and understanding when it's someone else's relative who messes up. Think back to when you were a kid. Other kids' mothers' weird behavior didn't bother you. But let your own mother do the least silly thing and you were embarrassed to tears."

Melissa nodded.

The door to the bedroom swung open. "Isn't it time for

lunch?" Darlene asked. "I'm starved."

"Sure thing." Melissa rose and headed to the kitchen. Could I look at Darlene as someone else's mother? Distance myself enough to be objective? As she pulled the bread sack open, she heard Darlene.

"How nice of you to join us for lunch."

"The pleasure is mine," Tyce replied.

"We'll be having clam chowder and salad. Melissa always fixes clam chowder on Friday."

Melissa waited for Tyce to correct Darlene on the day of the week. This was only Thursday. Instead she heard him say, "Clam chowder sounds good."

With a sigh of resignation Melissa shoved the bologna back in the refrigerator and opened the cupboard to find a can of clam chowder.

"Anything I can do to help you in there?" Tyce called.

"Nope. I'm doing fine." She dumped the premix salad into a bowl while the microwave heated the soup.

"What are your plans for this weekend?" Tyce asked Darlene.

"I haven't given that much thought."

"Weatherman says it will be nice."

"Actually," Melissa said as she brought dishes to the table, "I planned to surprise Mother with a trip to Turner."

"Sorry, didn't mean to spoil your surprise."

"Why didn't you say something?" Darlene frowned and raised a hand to fuss with her hair. "I can't possibly be ready to go. Oh my." She rose from the chair and shuffle-thumped her way back to the bedroom.

"Maybe I better go before I cause more trouble." Tyce looked repentant.

"Oh, no. I have clam chowder ready, and you better help eat it because it's not Friday."

She was surprised when instead of responding, Tyce asked, "What are you going to do in Turner?"

She hesitated only a fraction of a second. "Mother told me

Father wrote letters to me as a child. She never showed them to me. I think she may have saved them, and I want to see if I can find them. There's a room full of stuff in the old house."

"Need any help searching?" He'd come to stand close. She could smell his musk cologne, and her heartbeat picked up its tempo. She looked into brown eyes that seemed to reach her very soul.

"You might end up keeping Darlene company while I look."

She couldn't believe how important his answer was to her. It seemed he searched her face forever before his low voice answered, "If that's what you need, it's fine with me."

His hands reached for her upper arms and drew her close. "I wouldn't do this for just anyone." The twinkle in his eye sent thrills from her stomach to her chest and back. Like steel to a magnet she pressed against him. His head came down and their lips touched.

"That chowder ready?" Darlene called from the bedroom doorway.

❧

Friday evening traffic inched its way out of Seattle. Tyce sat behind the wheel of his Ford Taurus, and Darlene sat beside him. Melissa rode in the back seat, sharing it with Petey's cage.

Melissa wasn't sure she'd made the right choice in letting Tyce drive, but it was too late now to change her mind. She closed her eyes and willed each muscle to relax. She shrugged her shoulders to try and ward off the tension creeping up the back of her neck.

An overnight bag was all she'd packed, but Darlene had two suitcases. They'd almost gotten into a shouting match over whether to take Petey. Darlene simply sat down and refused to budge until Melissa gave in. Melissa felt like she was dealing with a two-year-old throwing a temper tantrum. The only difference was she could pick up a child and insist things be done her way.

Melissa's eyes flew open, and she stared at the back of Darlene's head. What was she thinking? Had she sat down to wait out Melissa's refusal to take Petey? Did she feel Melissa was the stubborn one? The unreasonable one?

It was close to ten when they pulled into Beverly's driveway and nearing eleven when Melissa plopped down on Beverly and Charles' bed. She was bone weary, but her mind kept thinking about her father's letters. Could she find them? What would they say?

❧

The sound of footsteps woke Melissa. The clock showed seven-thirty A.M.

"Beverly! You awake?" Darlene's question accompanied the whack of her cane against the door. "You better get up. There's a man in the kitchen."

Melissa threw the covers back and shivered at the morning chill. She realized they'd been so tired last night no one had thought to turn up the heat. The cane whacked again, and she hurried to open the door.

"Mother, I'm sure it's all right. It's probably Tyce."

Darlene's bewilderment was evident in the narrow-eyed look she gave Melissa. "Where's Beverly?"

"She's still in England. Remember, we drove down from Seattle last night."

Melissa watched for the questioning look to leave her mother's eyes. It hurt to see the doubt, the befuddled expression.

twelve

Tyce had a box of pancake mix sitting on the kitchen counter. "I found this in the cupboard. Doesn't seem to be much else to eat."

"I never even thought about bringing food. Probably the smart thing to do would be go out for breakfast. It would be a lot less hassle than shopping and carrying it back here to eat." Melissa pulled the robe she'd found in Beverly's closet tighter around her. "Besides, I'm too excited to eat. I want to get to the house and start looking for those letters."

"I can understand that. However, if you don't want to listen to my stomach rumble all morning you'll take pity and let me have some breakfast."

Melissa's laugh echoed through the rooms. Tyce realized it was the first time he'd heard her sound really happy. She had a great laugh. It crinkled the corners of her eyes and softened the expression around her mouth. The effect was dazzling.

"I'll run upstairs and see how Mother's doing. We should be ready in about twenty minutes. Can you wait that long?"

"I'll try to survive."

There weren't many eating choices in Turner. Melissa directed Tyce to a small family type restaurant. Tyce checked over the menu and settled on a short stack with sausage and two over-easy eggs. "I'll take decaf with that."

Darlene ordered a bowl of oatmeal. "You really should get oatmeal," she informed Melissa. "You don't eat nearly enough for breakfast."

Tyce watched Melissa skim over the menu. "I suppose I should." But when she handed the menu back to the waitress, she said, "Orange juice, please."

The waitress waited with poised pen. With a puzzled look she asked, "Will there be something else?"

"No, thank you."

"Be right back with your coffee." She picked up the extra place setting from the table and headed toward the kitchen.

The silence around the table began to pick at Tyce's nerves. What could he say that wouldn't set the two women at odds? He'd love to hear more about Melissa's childhood, but that subject was loaded.

"How long have you lived in Turner?" he finally asked Darlene.

"My folks moved here when I was ten. We bought one of those old farmhouses out toward Aumsville. My brothers thought it was great. They could finally have the dogs and horses they wanted."

Darlene paused, and Tyce decided she'd come to the end of her story.

The waitress showed up with their order, and it looked delicious. He glanced at Melissa. "Shall I bless it?"

"Yes."

"Lord, we thank You for providing this food and all good gifts. We ask for Your protective hand to be on us today. Help us that all we do and say may be pleasing to You. Amen."

"Amen," Melissa echoed.

"You know, I really hated that farm."

Darlene's statement caught Tyce just as he put the first bite of sausage into his mouth. He chewed and swallowed. Before he could comment, Melissa spoke.

"I remember driving out past Grandpa's place after he died. I always wished he'd lived long enough for me to remember going there."

"You and your dad." There was nothing complimentary in Darlene's tone. "Why, the minute he found out I'd inherited that farm he was all for moving out of town and back there. Can you imagine? He knew I never liked it."

"I didn't know you owned Grandpa's farm. Do you still own it?"

"Goodness no. I sold it as fast as I could. Franklin was furious when he found out."

"You didn't let Dad know you were selling it?"

"I knew your father would drag me back there if I kept it. I couldn't let that happen. The reason I married him was to get off the farm." Darlene became preoccupied with eating her oatmeal.

Melissa felt like her world had taken on the consistency of quicksand. Every new revelation from Darlene sucked her deeper down. Had there ever been any happiness in her family?

&

They pulled into the driveway of Darlene's house about nine-thirty. Melissa looked at the ancient structure with its peeling paint. Growing up, it had seemed like a big house. Big and fine. Not as nice as the banker's, but respectable. Over the years, the elements had tarnished its image.

The broad front porch still held a double swing. After a look at the rusty chains, Melissa decided not to trust her weight on it.

Darlene fumbled in her purse for the front door key. Then they moved into the hall with the open staircase leading to the upstairs bedrooms. It had the damp, musty smell of six months' standing empty. No one had bothered to put dust covers over the old furniture. Melissa trailed her finger along the edge of the hall tree leaving a clear line.

"What's first?" Tyce asked. He moved to stand in the archway leading off the hall into the dining room.

"I'll go up and start searching." Melissa turned to Darlene. "Do you have any idea where you stored my letters from Daddy?" She didn't know why she bothered to ask again. She'd brought up the question twice before. The first time Darlene said she didn't keep them. But later she talked about a shoebox in the closet where she'd hidden them. Which memory was accurate?

Now Darlene said, "They were in the bottom drawer of my dresser. But that was before Beverly packed my stuff."

"Beverly! Beverly knew about my letters?" Then another thought popped into Melissa's mind. "Did Beverly get letters from Daddy? Did you give them to her?" *Of course, Daddy would have written to us both. How could I be so dense?*

"You just don't understand."

"I'm trying to."

"There were letters for both you girls."

Melissa clinched her teeth to keep from speaking. Maybe Darlene would tell her the truth now.

"I'm tired of standing. Can't we find some chairs to sit on?"

Tyce whipped out his handkerchief and swished it across the seats of a couple of dining room chairs. A dust cloud hovered in the sunlight slanting through the window.

"Oops, maybe that wasn't such a good idea."

Melissa pinched her nose to keep from sneezing.

Tyce moved a chair so Darlene could sit. "Here you are."

"I miss living here. Look, there's my mother's wall clock above the buffet. Do you remember winding it as a child?" Darlene looked from the clock to Melissa.

"I don't believe I was ever allowed to touch that clock."

"No, maybe not. I guess I remember winding it when I was young. It hung between the two windows in the living room on the farm. It was quite fancy for its time. You only had to wind it every seven days. We wound it every Saturday night."

Obviously, Darlene had forgotten they were talking about the letters. Melissa couldn't get up the energy to ask again. "Give a yell if you need me. I'll be upstairs."

The third step creaked and so did the seventh. She recalled that if she wanted to sneak up or down she had to remember to skip the squeaky steps. Not much had changed in the house. Family photos still lined the stairwell. Her maternal grandparents stood in front of the old farmhouse. A picture of Darlene, Beverly, and Melissa had been taken the day

Beverly started first grade.

Had Beverly known even then about the letters? Was that part of her superior, know-it-all attitude? It hurt to think about it. A heavy pressure pushed against Melissa's chest, squeezing tears into her eyes. She turned her back to the photo gallery and hastened on to the back bedroom where, through the years, unused furniture, boxes of books, and mementos had found a place. To find a small bundle of letters in all this clutter seemed a daunting task.

The first few boxes held knickknacks that Beverly must have stored when getting Darlene ready to move in with her. Another box held Christmas cards. Melissa opened the first card. The date was 1998 and signed by a friend of Darlene's. Melissa reached for another then decided against it. If she got started, she could waste an hour or so reading old Christmas greetings. Sometime it might be interesting, but she had a more important task right now.

Dust floated in the air. Melissa sneezed. She shoved an old card table out of her way so she could get to the window. The fresh air rushed in as she shoved up the sash. Goose bumps popped out on her bare arms, and she shivered.

The room, which had been stale and chilly, switched to fresh and cold. If Melissa planned to work here much longer she would need a sweater. She should check up on how Darlene and Tyce were getting along. It had been awfully quiet downstairs.

Just for fun, she skipped the seventh and third steps and crept into the hall. What would it have been like to live here as a child with her father present? What could she remember? Did he laugh much? She peeked into the dining room where Tyce and Darlene had a deck of cards spread out on the corner of the table.

Tyce glanced up and smiled with a questioning raised eyebrow.

Melissa shook her head.

Darlene played her card seemingly unaware of the exchange.

Melissa slipped on down the hall to the kitchen. Bless Tyce for keeping Mother occupied.

Out the kitchen window she looked into the overgrown backyard. The old oak tree stood to one side. A memory stirred. Her father had attached a tire swing to the lower branch. It was long gone, but she remembered it. Melissa closed her eyes and reached back in time for a picture. *Yes! Dad pushed me on that tire.* For a minute she soared. But she couldn't see him. She couldn't hear his voice. All pictures of him had long since disappeared.

She pulled a glass from the cupboard and turned on the faucet. A deep gurgling sound came from the faucet but no water. With disgust she replaced the glass. Of course, the water had been turned off when Darlene moved out.

Maybe she should go to the store for some soda. But she didn't want to take the time. If she was going to know anything about her father, she had to find those letters.

Rummaging through Darlene's closet Melissa found an old sweater. Fortunately, it had been very large on Darlene. Now she'd get back to searching. But the dresser caught her eye as she headed out of the room. Hadn't Darlene said she'd kept the letters in a bottom drawer once? Of course, she'd also said she'd thrown them away.

Melissa started with the top drawer. It was empty. The next one held only an old nightgown that should have been tossed ages ago. She was finding the leftovers Beverly had disdained to move with Darlene.

She'd left the bottom drawer to last. Now she hesitated. Could the long-lost letters really be there? With a tug, she revealed a bare drawer. The disappointment hit her in the pit of her stomach. How could she have set herself up like that? If they ever had been here, Beverly would have removed them. Would she destroy them?

"Hey, need any help?"

Melissa whirled at the sound of Tyce's voice. Her heart pounded. Wrapped up in her own little drama, she hadn't heard Tyce come up the stairs.

"Oops, didn't mean to startle you. Guess you haven't found anything yet."

"Not yet." Melissa closed the drawer. "There're a couple big boxes in the other room you can help me move if you have time."

"Darlene is taking a nap on the sofa. So I should have a little time to help."

"You've been a big help already."

They moved to the storage room. Boxes had been stacked head high along one wall. Melissa had looked for some identification, but nothing seemed marked.

"Guess I should start here on this end nearest the door."

Together they lowered a large box to the card table Melissa had set up for a work area. It beat sitting on the floor or bending over. The first box contained old linens. She glanced through them thinking she should just toss them. "I suppose I should mark the contents of each box. Then we won't have to guess the next time we look for something. What I need is a heavy black marking pen."

"I think I've got something that will do in my briefcase out in the car."

A half dozen boxes later, she'd identified old toys, Christmas ornaments, plastic flowers, books, and craft materials.

"I didn't know Mother was such a hoarder," Melissa said, viewing a cracked glass candleholder.

"It comes from the generation that went through the Depression, and they passed it on to their kids. They didn't throw away anything that might be used again. I know my grandparents were that way." Tyce reached for another box. "Actually, I'd say it's one of the best things you have going for you."

"What do you mean?" Melissa pressed her hands into the

middle of her back and stretched.

"The possibility of those letters still being here goes up exponentially with the number of boxes stored away. It means no one's been in here cleaning up and tossing stuff for years."

"Hey, that sounds right. The stuff from twenty-five years ago should be at the bottom of this stack, and it doesn't look like it's been touched."

"Want to start at the far end?" Tyce's crooked grin lit up his face.

"Yeah. Let's see how to do this. We can recognize the boxes we've already looked in by the writing on them. We can move these next boxes off to the side and start at the bottom." In her enthusiasm, Melissa grabbed a box and shoved it toward Tyce. "Put it over there." She pointed with her chin.

In a few minutes, the bottom row of boxes was all exposed, and Melissa sat in front of them. "I'm so excited I'm almost shaking. I'm actually beginning to believe I'll find Dad's letters." She smiled up at Tyce, but the smile faded as she looked at his face. "What's the matter?"

Tyce shook his head. "I just don't want you getting too excited. There's a very real possibility your mother destroyed the letters when they arrived. Don't get your hopes too high."

"I know you're right. But I have this feeling."

"Just remember, we can look for your Dad even if the letters aren't here."

"Right!" She made a mental note that he'd said "we." Was she depending on him too much? She mustn't take advantage of his friendship. For that's all their relationship would ever be.

"I'll go down and look in on Darlene. Make sure she's still resting all right."

"Okay. You know where to find me if you need me." She heard his retreating steps as she opened the next box. Inside were a number of smaller boxes. The first one she pulled out contained empty perfume bottles. "I'll bet these have some antique value." She opened one and brought it to her nose. A faint floral scent escaped. She recapped the bottle and went to the next box. The side read, *Sears and Roebuck, size 10 ½.*

Melissa read the words twice before it dawned on her. The only person in the family who could have owned a size 10½ shoe would have been her father. She was holding something that had actually belonged to him. No matter what was in it she was going to keep the box.

The lid fell to one side as she looked in. Lined up on a card were a half dozen lures. Fishing line wound around a short willow stick. A few sinkers and bobbers lay in the bottom.

Melissa couldn't stop the tears. She hugged the box to her and wept. Her Dad had given these to her, she was sure. But she didn't remember putting them away. Probably it happened the same day she broke her willow pole. She could remember destroying it.

thirteen

A light snore came from the direction of the sofa. Tyce tip-toed into the room. He'd prefer Darlene to continue her nap for at least another half hour. By then Melissa would have looked through the bottom row of boxes. He'd like to be up there when she found the letters. But a tug-of-war raged between what he'd like and what he figured would be best for Melissa. She probably needed time by herself.

But what if she doesn't find the letters? he argued. *She'll need moral support. Or a shoulder to cry on.* That thought brought ambivalence. What was he thinking? Of course, he wanted her to find the letters. A celebrating hug was just as good as a comforting one. Maybe better.

Let's face it, old boy. You're no longer content with your life as it is. At the earliest possible moment, you're going to let Melissa know you want her to be part of it.

He let his mind drift. He pictured her sprawled at his feet, wet bangs dripping down her face. He shocked himself by wiping the rain from the tip of her nose.

When did it happen? When did he fall in love?

Even as he thought about it he knew the timing wasn't right. Melissa needed to untangle a lot of family knots. Not the least of them was finding her father.

"Rest on," he whispered to Darlene and headed toward the stairs.

He could hear the sobs as he reached the head of the stairs. He hesitated with indecision, then quickened his pace.

Melissa sat huddled on the floor, rocking gently.

Despite all his self-talk, he dropped beside her and gathered her close. Her sobs gradually slowed. He leaned his cheek against her hair and inhaled the herbal scent of shampoo.

When the sobs slowed, he whispered, "Want to tell me about it?"

In response, she straightened and held out the box she'd been clutching to her breast. Tyce looked at the fishing gear, trying to find the cause of so many tears. He didn't get it. "No letters?"

She shook her head. "But look." She raised the box for his inspection.

He was looking and it made no sense. Then it dawned on him. "These belonged to your father."

"Sort of. He gave them to me when I was five. See, he put them in one of his own shoeboxes. I actually found something belonging to my father."

It was such a small crumb, Tyce felt like crying himself. But she wouldn't leave empty-handed. Maybe this was good enough.

"Melissa." The call came from downstairs. "Melissa, you up there?"

"Yes, Mother. Be right there." She placed the shoebox on the card table and swiped at the wet blotches on her cheeks. Then, as though she couldn't bear to be separated from it, she picked the box up and took it with her.

"There you are. You have company."

"Surprise!" Gilbert stuck his head around the corner of the dining room arch. "I saw a car parked outside and decided to investigate. Didn't want some stranger breaking into your house."

"That was thoughtful. I was upstairs and didn't hear you knock."

"I didn't knock. Didn't want to give burglars a chance to get away out the back door while I was waiting at the front." Gilbert shook his head until Tyce thought it would come loose from his neck.

"That could have been dangerous, walking in on armed strangers."

Gilbert's head stopped shaking. He swallowed convulsively, causing his Adam's apple to bob. "Wow! I never thought about that. Guess it's a good thing it was just you guys." His nervous laugh bounced off the walls.

"Come on in." Darlene took hold of Gilbert's sleeve. "We might as well sit down."

Tyce watched Melissa's face. Her look said this was the last thing she wanted to do. There were still unopened boxes, and she didn't want to waste a minute sitting and chatting.

But he knew she was too polite to rush off. So they all filed into the living room where Darlene had napped on the sofa.

"The house hasn't changed in all these years," Gilbert said. He pointed to a faded landscape hanging above the fireplace. "That picture's been there forever."

"Hey." Tyce leaned toward Gilbert. "I thought you'd be in California by now on that new job."

"The company decided to hold off on the move until the first of next year. So I have two more months here in Turner."

"Guess your mother is pleased about that," Darlene said. "You raise kids until they're old enough to be good company, then they move away. Did you know Beverly has gone to Europe?"

"Yeah, I knew that, Mrs. Wilabee." Gilbert squirmed on his chair like an embarrassed kid.

Out of the corner of his eye, Tyce saw Melissa sneak a look at her watch. He had a choice. He could sit here and politely listen to this inane conversation, or he could put them all out of their misery.

"Sure was nice of you to check out the situation when you saw the strange car." Tyce rose and stretched out a hand toward Gilbert.

Gilbert immediately got up to shake Tyce's hand.

"Melissa has quite a bit of sorting left to do upstairs, and since the electricity is off she'd best get it done while there's still some daylight left."

Gilbert pointed at the shoebox Melissa still clutched in both hands. "Is that some of the stuff you're sorting?"

"Yes."

"What is it?"

"Memories from my childhood. If you'll all excuse me, I will get back to work."

"Can I help?" Gilbert looked as eager as a puppy.

"That's a very generous offer," Tyce said. "We really hate to leave Darlene down here by herself, and the stairs are too difficult for her to climb. If you have an hour or so to visit with Darlene it would be a great help. There's a deck of cards in the dining room."

Without giving Gilbert a chance to respond, Tyce touched Melissa's elbow and steered her toward the stairs. When they reached the privacy of the storage room, Melissa spoke.

"You have a devious side I wasn't aware of."

"Too cruel?"

"We'd better ask Gilbert to join us for supper to make up for it."

"That bad, huh?"

Her smile took the sting out of her words. "Downright mean."

As Melissa finished with one box, Tyce stored it on the far side of the room. Soon there were only two boxes left to complete the search. Melissa had moved the card table over under the window to catch the fading light. Tyce deposited the boxes and stood back.

Without hesitation Melissa flipped the flaps open. It only took a minute to see that neither carton contained the letters.

"So, I guess she destroyed them." Melissa closed the boxes.

"Looks like it."

"Maybe it would have been better if I'd never known about them. Now I have this hole. A dull ache that says something precious is lost forever."

"I don't know how all this will turn out. But I think just

knowing your father cared enough to write is an important step in healing the chasm between you."

"I can't find the letters. What if I can't find him?"

"Don't borrow tomorrow's troubles. God'll give you a new supply of strength when you need it."

"That sounds pretty profound. Maybe you should have been a preacher."

Tyce's laughter rumbled from deep in his chest. "You are easily impressed." He moved the final box and folded the card table. "How about we go and see about getting some food?"

They chose to return to the family restaurant for dinner. Gilbert chatted about local news, reminding Melissa of friends from school. "Hey, look who just walked in." Gilbert stood and waved his hands above his head. "Jeff. Over here."

A tall, lanky man sauntered to the table. "Hi, Gilbert. Hello, Melissa." He nodded his head in Darlene's direction. "Mrs. Wilabee."

"Won't you join us?" Darlene asked. "Pull up that other chair."

Melissa wasn't thrilled at having dinner with the former high school basketball star. She remembered him as a conceited bore. But that was years ago, and he'd probably matured. "Jeff, this is my friend, Tyce Nelson. Tyce, Jeff Damson."

Tyce stood and shook hands. "Nice to meet you."

"So, what ya doing back here in our little burg?" Jeff directed his question to Melissa.

Melissa groped for a quick but evasive answer. She hadn't come prepared for an inquisition.

"She's searching for something in the old house," Gilbert volunteered.

"I always thought your house had character." Jeff turned to Darlene. "You're living up with Beverly now, aren't you? Is the house for sale?"

"Young man, I'll be back in my own house as soon as my leg is well."

"Glad to hear it." He turned his attention back to Melissa. "Nice to see you again. You're looking good. Maybe I'll see you around again."

The look in his eye and his tone of voice sent heat waves up Melissa's cheeks. She nodded but couldn't think of a thing to say as he headed over to the counter to speak to the waitress.

Gilbert leaned forward and confided. "He and Carolyn have been seeing each other. You know he married Joan right after high school. She died of cancer a year ago. They never had any kids."

"I didn't know." Melissa realized she hadn't kept in touch with any of the kids from school.

Their food came, and Gilbert blessed it. "This is good," he said around a mouthful of the house specialty, a thick slab of roast beef with mashed potatoes drowning in gravy. "I don't eat out much. Usually stay home and eat with Mom and Dad."

The comment didn't seem to need an answer so Melissa retreated into her own thoughts. Could there be anything else of her father's stashed away in the house? There was a desk with lots of pigeonholes in the living room. What was in it? She'd have to wait until tomorrow. It was too dark to do any more searching tonight.

"Are you going to sort more stuff tomorrow?" Gilbert asked.

Melissa sensed that he wanted to ask more. Like, what are you looking for? What's in the shoebox? She couldn't decide whether she wanted him to know about the letters or not. Would it be fair to her mother to let the whole town know what she'd done years ago?

It surprised Melissa that she should be concerned about what people thought about her mother. At times she felt like shouting to the world what a horrible thing she'd done. Then she would open her Bible and read things like, "Love your enemies. Do good to those who persecute you."

"If we have time, I'd like to go back and look some more after church tomorrow. We don't want to get too late a start heading back to Seattle."

Tyce spoke up for the first time since Jeff left. "There'll be several hours before we need to head back." He turned to Darlene. "Do you mind getting in late?"

"I don't think I'll go back." Darlene toyed with her napkin, folding and unfolding it. "Beverly will be back in a couple days, and there's no sense making the trip twice. Now, don't argue. I've made up my mind."

"Then it doesn't matter what time we head back. Melissa will have plenty of time to do more looking."

Tyce's statement left Melissa with her mouth hanging open. She watched Darlene reach out and pat Tyce's hand.

Has everyone gone crazy?

The absurdity of it all didn't seem to reach Gilbert. "Just what are you looking for?"

"Mother put away some of my things years ago. I'd like to find them."

Gilbert grinned. "Mom used to do that. She'd threaten if we didn't play nice she'd take away a certain toy. When we got to fighting, she'd take the toy and put it on the top shelf in the kitchen cupboard. That worked until Frank and I got big enough to climb up on the kitchen counter and get it back."

Melissa never thought of looking in the kitchen. "Tyce, do you have a flashlight in the car?"

"I have one of those big emergency lights."

"Good. Is everyone done eating? I want to go back to the house tonight."

"Don't you want to order dessert first?" Gilbert looked wistfully at the display of pies and cakes in their glass case.

"No." Melissa scooted her chair back and reached for her coat.

Tyce spoke softly over her shoulder. "Don't get your hopes high. The chances are slim."

❧

The flashlight beam bounced off the kitchen walls and up to the old-fashioned twelve-foot ceiling. One wall was covered with cupboards reaching to within a foot of the water-stained ceiling. Melissa couldn't remember anything being kept on those top shelves.

"Wow! Those cupboards are high. Glad we didn't have such high ceilings. Frank and I never would have gotten our toys back." Gilbert's bray echoed through the empty house.

Melissa shoved a kitchen chair next to the counter. With a steadying hand from Tyce and a warning from Gilbert to be careful, she climbed onto the Formica. She wasn't tall enough to make the flashlight beam reach to the back of the top shelf.

"I need to stack something on the counter. Gilbert, there's an old set of encyclopedias in the living room. Bring a half dozen."

When the books were in place, Melissa gripped a cabinet edge and stepped up. Gilbert and Tyce both stood with their arms raised, ready to catch her should she slip.

"There's something back there!" Melissa's voice rose. "Hurry, get me some more books."

"I don't think that would be safe," Tyce said. "Come on down, and I'll see if I can reach them."

"Hey, I've got six inches on you both." Gilbert stretched his arm to full length. "And you never saw anybody with longer arms. Remember they called me monkey in school 'cause I could bend over and drag my knuckles on the ground."

"He's right, Melissa. Let Gilbert get what's up there."

Reluctantly, Melissa climbed down and handed the light to Gilbert.

"Here goes." Gilbert stepped easily onto the chair, then the counter, and atop the books. The flashlight reached into the dark recess. "You've got cobwebs up here."

"Never mind. Bring out the package I saw."

"Ta-da!" Gilbert placed it in Melissa's hands.

It was wrapped in newspaper and covered with years of dust.

fourteen

The package lay in Melissa's lap as she sat in the middle of Beverly's bed. She had ignored her mother's "Well, open it" and Gilbert's "Do you know what's in it?" There was no way she would open it in front of everyone.

Tyce had bustled everyone out to the car. With determined efficiency, he'd taken control. "Come on. It's getting late. We'll see you at church in the morning, Gilbert."

No one said another word about the package.

Now, as Melissa sat staring at the package, she was torn between the desire to tear it open and the fear of discovering there weren't any letters inside.

The letters would prove whether her father loved her or not. They'd also show the length to which her mother would go to punish her ex-husband. Even to destroying a child's love for her father. And here Melissa sat in Beverly's room on Beverly's bed—Beverly, who all these years had probably known about the letters.

Suddenly Melissa didn't want to think about the people in her life, the people who made her feel the way she did inside— sad and angry. She shivered. The room had grown cold.

A light tap on the door was followed by a whisper. "You all right in there?"

Melissa nodded, then realized Tyce couldn't see her. "I'm okay." The Lord would have to forgive her for that outright lie. She wasn't okay. She'd never been less okay in her life.

"May I come in?"

"Yes." She set the package on the bedspread beside her. It had taken on a life of its own. It represented all the good and evil she'd ever known.

Tyce stuck his head around the door. "It's after midnight, and I could see there was a light still on in here."

"Midnight?" Melissa looked at her watch. Two hours. She couldn't believe how long she'd sat staring at the package.

"Doesn't look like you've opened it."

She shook her head.

"Twenty-five years. I guess another hour or two won't matter."

What started out as a smile on Melissa's face crumpled into tears.

Tyce crossed the room in two long strides and gathered her into his arms. Without speaking he rocked her gently. The tears didn't last long. She brushed them aside.

"Twenty-five years!" Her voice came out weak and scratchy. "It's time to put an end to this." She snatched up the package and yanked on the string. The brittle paper crumbled and a dozen envelopes fell out. They were all addressed to Miss Melissa Wilabee in neat handwriting she never remembered seeing.

Her hands flew to her mouth. "My letters!" Her heart pounded so hard she felt it shake her whole body.

"Look." She picked up an envelope. "It's never been opened. I supposed Mother had read them."

"They're just waiting for you." Tyce rose from the bed. "I'll leave you to your reading."

She caught his arm. "Don't go."

"Are you sure?"

Melissa looked deep into his questioning eyes. She'd never been so sure of anything before. The letters had unlocked a part of her heart she'd closed to all intruders. "I'm sure. If you want to?" she added. She hadn't realized how much his answer would mean.

"Thank you." He returned to his spot on the bedspread. "I would love to share this discovery with you."

She gathered the envelopes and meticulously sorted them

by the dated postmark. "This letter arrived the week of my sixth birthday. Daddy would have been gone about three months if I remember right."

Running a finger under the flap, she opened the first envelope. It contained a single sheet of writing paper with a blue flower in the upper left-hand corner.

My dear Melissa,
 You will be six years old when you read this. I shall miss giving you a kiss for each year. The teddy bear I found in a little store in California. I call him Cubby. But you can name him whatever you like.

Melissa stopped reading and pressed her hand to her chest to try and slow her pounding heart. Her mother's sins had just doubled. "I never got the teddy bear."

     ❧

The pain in Melissa's eyes was almost more than Tyce could stand. How could a mother do such a thing to a child?

"Your mother must have been awfully angry with your father. I would guess she did what she did to hurt him, not you."

He watched Melissa smooth out the folds in the letter. "Perhaps you're right."

She was hurting so badly Tyce ached for her. There wasn't a lot he could say to her. He didn't know all the circumstances. Had Darlene thought it was in the best interest of her girls to cut off communications with their father? What could you do about such misguided love?

"I doubt parents ever think of their children first when they're caught up in the turmoil of their own lives." Tyce waited a moment to see if Melissa would respond. "Did you catch what your mother said when you asked about the farm?"

At that, Melissa looked up from the letter. "I'm not sure I get the connection. What does the farm have to do with my letters?"

"Maybe it explains a lot of Darlene's guilt."

"Guilt? You think she feels guilty?"

"She said she married your father to get off the farm. That may have been a stronger reason for marriage than her love for him. She's lived with that guilt. And guilt often makes you strike out at the person you've wronged."

"You're saying Mother withheld these letters to punish Father."

"Something like that."

"If she'd already betrayed my father by marrying him for the wrong reasons, why did she want to continue to punish him?"

"Maybe she couldn't forgive herself." Tyce didn't know if he was helping Melissa cope or just muddying the waters.

"Is this one of those, 'It's easier for you to see because she's not your mother'?"

Tyce laughed out loud and was glad to see a smile crease Melissa's face. "You're catching on."

Melissa began to read again.

You will be starting first grade in September. When you learn to write, I would love to receive a letter from you in your own handwriting. Maybe until then your mother can write a letter for you.

I love you always,
Daddy

"How it must have hurt him to never hear from me. And yet he continued to write."

"It takes a lot to push away real love."

Melissa carefully refolded the letter and put it into its envelope. She stifled a yawn.

Immediately Tyce stood up. "Way past your bedtime. Think you can sleep?"

"I doubt it, but I guess I better try."

He leaned over and left a lingering kiss on her forehead.

"Thank you for letting me share this with you." He left, quietly closing her bedroom door behind him. *The possibility of getting any sleep myself is remote. I'll lie down and rest. If I can't sleep, I can always spend the time in prayer.*

❧

Melissa almost called Tyce back. But it was the middle of the night, and she should let him get some sleep. Besides, she needed to do this on her own. Now wasn't the time to start leaning on someone else. There had never been anyone for her to lean on—not Mother, not Beverly.

She picked up the next envelope and slid her finger under the flap. *If only I'd gotten Father's letters. How it would have changed my childhood. Yeah, and if wishes were horses, beggars would ride.* Somewhere her mother had picked up that quote and used it whenever the girls began whining and wishing things were different.

My Sweet Melissa,
　　Merry Christmas. I've found a job here in California. I won't have any snow to help celebrate the season, but maybe you will. You should get my package in a couple days. Be a good girl and don't open it until Christmas.

I love you always,
Daddy

Melissa threw herself back against the pillows, letting the tears flow. It crossed her mind that sometime soon she should be running out of tears. Where did they all come from? She flopped onto her stomach and pulled the pillow close. Hugging it fiercely, she began to imagine a childhood playing with her father's gifts.

❧

Melissa was chilled all the way through. She reached to pull the covers up and realized she lay on top of them. By the light on Beverly's nightstand she looked at the clock—it said four.

Stiff and shivering, she crawled under the blankets, not bothering to undress. She clicked off the light. It hurt her eyes.

Three hours later Melissa awoke with a start. She wasn't dreaming. She had found her father's letters. She looked across the bedspread. Her rolling and tossing had scattered them, but all twelve of them were there.

Sunshine streamed in across the bed. She'd never gotten around to pulling the curtain last night, and she could see blue sky stretching beyond the large cedar. How could a morning seem so normal? There should be bells ringing—a trumpet fanfare. She reached for the bathrobe lying on the foot of the bed and wrapped it around her shoulders.

A flock of black-capped chickadees landed in the shrubbery. Several checked out a feeder hanging from a low cedar branch. No one had filled it since Beverly and Charles left, so the birds moved on.

One by one, she lay the envelopes in a line beside her. They marched across the spread in a file six feet long. Melissa grinned, realizing that strung out this way, they were taller than she was. They were as tall as her father. With that thought she frowned. Was that true? A simple thing like knowing how tall your own father was had been denied her.

The third envelope contained the same flowered paper.

Dear Melissa,

I went to an Easter sunrise service this morning. I thought of you in your new Easter dress. You must have looked very pretty. Did you go to church?

If you can find time, I would love to hear from you.

I love you always,
Daddy

P.S. I'm going to be moving in a couple weeks. I'll send you a new address.

One after the other, Melissa read the letters. They covered a period of not quite three years. It dawned on her that her father had given up hearing from her about the same time she gave up expecting him to come home.

The sound of Darlene's shuffle-thump brought Melissa back to the present. The letters had raised a lot of questions. Should Melissa confront Darlene about the presents she'd been denied? Or just skip it and get on with locating her father? Did Darlene know the letters were in the kitchen all along?

It was too bad this hadn't come out in the open five years ago. Then Darlene wouldn't have dementia as an excuse for her poor memory. But it was the dementia that had finally revealed the truth.

Melissa wrapped the letters in a piece of white tissue paper she pulled from the bottom of Beverly's drawer. It gave her a certain satisfaction to scatter all the carefully folded nighties as she whipped out the drawer lining. Revenge. It struck her how petty she was behaving. But she closed the drawer and left it topsy-turvy.

She opened her overnighter and pulled out clean clothes, then tucked the letters in the bottom of the bag.

Refreshed from a shower, Melissa went in search of Tyce and her mother.

"Good morning." The late hour didn't seem to have bothered Tyce. He looked bright and smiling.

"Good morning." Melissa included them both in her greeting and realized Darlene was dressed ready for church.

"Are we going out for breakfast again?" Darlene asked.

"Sounds good to me. What about you, Melissa?"

Melissa nodded. Sleep, wake, shower, eat—it was all too ordinary. The world should have changed because she had changed.

More customers crowded into the little restaurant this morning. You could tell the ones who made eating Sunday breakfast there a habit. They called greetings back and forth. The women asked how the family was doing. The men slapped each other on the back. And they all glanced at the four strangers in their midst.

"Darlene? Is that you?" The woman wore too much makeup and a skirt several generations too short. "Haven't seen you out and about for a long time."

"Hello, Rosemary," Darlene said in recognition. "You remember my daughter, Melissa?"

Darlene played the perfect hostess. She didn't skip a beat. She introduced Tyce, making sure Rosemary was duly impressed with his credentials.

"Good to meet you." Rosemary excused herself and joined her own party.

The whole conversation left Melissa bewildered. How could Darlene be so together now and so befuddled at other times? She remembered Tyce had pulled information about dementia off the Web. She'd need to go back and look at it again. She'd tucked it away in a drawer at the time, thinking it had little to do with Darlene.

❧

Having decided she didn't need to search for anything else in the house, Melissa suggested they make an early afternoon start for Seattle. Nothing more was said about Darlene remaining in Turner. Obviously she had changed her mind or, more likely, forgotten she'd ever declared her intentions to stay.

It dawned on Melissa that Tyce had realized Darlene wouldn't likely remember her decision to stay, and that's why he just went along with it. Would she ever get to the point where she could consider Mother's speech and actions with such objectivity?

Monday after work Melissa drove to the senior center to pick Darlene up. When she'd dropped her off after lunch, Melissa took Mary aside and handed her a business card. "If Mother decides to make a break for it, I'd appreciate a call."

Mary nodded, her sparkling eyes acknowledging the conspiracy.

"Did you enjoy your card games?" Melissa helped Darlene out of the car and into the apartment building.

"Doris cheats."

"That's too bad."

"She's not very good at it—I always catch her."

"Maybe you can find someone else to play with."

"It doesn't matter. She loses anyway."

Melissa chuckled. For years, her mother had hosted a weekly bridge game. You had to be a pretty sharp player to beat her.

Petey greeted them with a raucous squawk.

"I think I'll rest a bit before supper." Darlene headed straight to the bedroom.

Melissa rummaged in her briefcase for a small notebook. She'd bought it at the college bookstore that morning. She spread her letters out on the dining table and recorded each place her father mentioned in his letters. He'd moved three times during the three-year period. But he'd remained in California. The last address was a P.O. box.

Why did he go to California? Melissa realized she didn't even know where her father grew up. Did he go home?

She gathered up her letters and notebook and placed them in a drawer. She could hardly wait for Darlene's nap to be over. There were a dozen questions she needed answers to.

Pulling out a box of Tuna Helper, she started supper. She clattered pans and turned the radio up, wondering how much noise it would take to get Darlene up.

The phone rang, and she waited until the third ring to pick it up. "Hello."

"Hi." Tyce's deep voice brought a special smile to her face. "Thought I'd check and see what's happening."

"All's quiet on the western front."

"Huh? Wasn't that a war story? Have you been in a fight?"

"I feel like this is just the calm before the storm."

"You're just full of clichés."

"Actually, I'm full of questions. I've realized I know practically nothing about Dad or his family. If I'm going to find him, I have to get some answers."

"Darlene doesn't know?"

"She's napping. I hoped the phone ringing would wake her up. Now that I've gotten started, I can't wait."

"What can I do to help?"

Old insecurities stirred. "You've been a big help already." She tried to make her words come out as thanks, but they sounded more like a dismissal. She needed to do this on her own. To rely on Tyce could lead to more problems than she already had.

The pause on the other end told her Tyce had heard the rejection.

"I'll keep in touch and see how you're doing. Have a good night."

The line went dead before she could respond. She closed her eyes and sighed. Rejection. It hurt to receive it or give it.

fifteen

"I asked Tyce how your trip to Turner went." Nancy paused in Melissa's office. "He thought maybe you'd like to give me the details yourself."

Melissa looked at the short, plump secretary waiting for an answer. Her thoughts whirled at the mention of Tyce. She'd slept poorly last night. And it was all his fault. "The trip was safe. Found what I was looking for."

"I'm sure glad I came to you for the details." From Nancy, it was the nearest thing to sarcasm you'd get.

"I don't mean to sound ungrateful." They were the wrong words, but Melissa didn't know how else to say it. "So much has happened. I need time to figure this all out." The words stumbled to a halt.

"You seem to have decided your friends can't help you anymore."

"That's not true. You are one of the best friends I've ever had. Some things I just have to work out on my own."

"On the surface that sounds fine—pull yourself up by your own bootstraps. Just be sure you don't shut out God as well as your friends."

"I'm not shutting out God. You know better than that."

"Just so you know better." Nancy came around the desk and gave Melissa a hug. "Don't be afraid to call on your friends. We want to help."

Five minutes after Nancy left the office, Melissa was still staring blankly at the papers on her desk. Life had suddenly gotten very complicated—she hated it. She couldn't stand messes. Clutter drove her crazy. When would it ever straighten out?

The answer to part of her problem was buried in Darlene's mind. Last night after supper when Melissa began to probe about her father, Darlene had simply refused to discuss him.

"After all these years," she'd said, "these years when I've taken care of you and your father was gone. . ." The sentence ended in sobs.

"Mother, I know you've been here for me all the time. That's not the point. Dad's a piece of my life that's been missing."

"And good riddance."

"I'm going to find him with or without your help." Melissa realized instantly her challenge was the wrong approach. Her intent wasn't to alienate her mother. "I'm sorry. I love you and don't want to hurt you. I hope you can understand why I'm doing this."

The phone on Melissa's desk rang and brought her back to the present. "Hello."

"Hi, Melissa." She'd recognize that nasal twang anywhere.

"Gilbert, what's up?"

"I was telling my folks about you finding the letters and—"

"How'd you know what I found? I don't remember saying what was in the package."

"Darlene told me while we were walking out to the cars. Was it a secret? I'm sorry if I spilled the beans."

"No, Gilbert. It's not a secret." *Mother recognized the package and knew I'd found Dad's letters!* She couldn't help but wonder if Darlene had known of their whereabouts all along.

"Sure glad to hear I didn't talk out of turn. My folks have always liked you, and they wanted to know how you were doing and why you were here in Turner. So we got to talking, and they began remembering stuff about your family. You know, they've known Darlene since she and Mom were in high school together. Don't think they were in the same class. Maybe Darlene was a year or two older."

"Gilbert." Melissa interrupted the torrent of words.

"Well, yeah. I guess you know all that. Why I called was to

let you know Mom and Dad said they'd be glad to talk to you about your father. Mom said it was such a nasty divorce that your mom might not like to talk about it. But you have a right to know. Folks here thought your dad got a raw deal. I don't remember him myself, of course. But Dad says he was an all right guy. Kind of felt sorry for him."

"Thank you," Melissa said when Gilbert paused for breath. "I guess there would be a lot of folks in Turner who remember my father. Tell your parents I appreciate the offer."

"Think you'll come back this weekend?" Eagerness raced over the phone line.

"Probably not. Two weekends in a row might be too much for Mother."

"Hadn't thought of that."

"I'll give you a call in a few days and let you know what I decide. Be sure and thank your folks. Bye."

Melissa mulled over the phone conversation. Did she want to dig into her family's past by discussing it with the town folks of Turner? It had never dawned on her before that the private affairs of her family were common knowledge around town.

But if they could help her locate her father, wouldn't it be worth it?

&

"That's quite a frown on your face." Nancy brought her lunch over and placed it on the table beside Tyce. "Worried about Melissa?"

Tyce nodded absentmindedly. "I don't know how to help her." He took another bite of cafeteria pizza.

"When I can't figure out what to do, I start making lists," Nancy said. "Melissa has three needs: physical, mental, and spiritual. Now under physical," Nancy said as she pulled out a small notepad and started writing, "let's put 'care of mother.' "

"Add 'searching for father.' "

"Both of those projects could be full-time." Nancy attacked

her salad, popping a bite into her mouth. Then she waved her fork in the air, punctuating each item she thought of. "Time, energy, money. They're all involved."

"We can't separate the physical, mental, and spiritual. This searching for her father has all three elements tied together in a knot that's going to be hard to unravel."

"Precisely." Nancy gave an extra jab with her fork. "That's one of the benefits of making lists. It helps you see how everything is interconnected."

"You mean if you can't figure which column to put it under, you know it's complicated?"

"That's certainly one way to look at it. But it helps me see that anything I do to help in one area will benefit all areas. You say you don't know how to help. If you can figure out one simple thing you can do to make Melissa's situation easier, you're actually doing a great deal to help."

"You two look serious." Tyce looked up to see Melissa standing next to Nancy holding her food tray.

Nancy slid her notepad out of the way and motioned for Melissa to join them.

Tyce saw the shadows under Melissa's eyes. She wasn't getting enough sleep. "Busy morning? I began to think you weren't going to make it down for lunch."

"Don't worry about me. I never miss a meal." Melissa's voice was a bit too bright.

In the silence that followed, Tyce thought, *But I do worry about you. According to Nancy's theory, if I can come up with one significant way to help, I can ease your whole load.*

"Where's Darlene?" Nancy dug into her slice of apple pie.

"The senior center had an outing this morning."

"Where to?"

"They took a vanload to tour the Frye Art Museum."

"I hope Darlene enjoys that."

Melissa nodded.

Tyce's mind searched for a solution. What kind of help

would Melissa accept? He tuned back in to what Melissa and Nancy were discussing in time to hear Nancy ask, "Won't she be tired?"

"What option do I have?" Melissa sounded defeated. "Leaving her alone at the apartment is really out of the question."

"Let's think about it."

Tyce expected Nancy to reach for her notepad and start making columns of possibilities. Instead, she closed her eyes in concentration. Without opening them she said, "One. Darlene will be very tired after her morning's outing. Two. You can't leave your office today because the state examiner is coming to go over the loan records."

"If it was any other day I could take work home and that would solve the problem."

"I could watch her," Tyce offered.

"I can't allow you to do that," Melissa objected.

Tyce looked at Nancy. "Did I ask for her permission?"

"Didn't seem that way to me."

Melissa wagged her head in surrender. "You guys are having way too much fun at my expense."

"Actually, no expense at all. Darlene-sitting is free."

Just then a couple dozen students came rushing into the cafeteria. "Class got out late," one called to a friend already eating his lunch. "Save me a seat."

During the commotion, Tyce studied Melissa. The strain of caring for Darlene showed in the slump of her shoulders. She was pushing her food around on the plate but hadn't eaten much. Maybe with Nancy's help he could coax Melissa into letting him carry some of her burden.

"Have I told you what great friends you two are? How can I ever thank you?"

Nancy patted her hand. "Just don't shut us out, and we'll try not to be too obnoxious or bossy or snoopy. Anything else you want to add, Tyce?"

"I was thinking of that scripture in 1 Peter. Chapter four,

I believe. It says not to be surprised, that there will be suffering. We'll be insulted for the name of Christ. That's not an exact quote. But it goes ahead and says don't suffer as a murderer or thief or even as a meddler."

"That's a good one. We'll definitely add meddler to the list."

"What time do we need to pick Darlene up?" Tyce glanced at his watch.

"The van is supposed to come back at one."

"Isn't your meeting at one-thirty?" Nancy asked. "That hardly gives you time to pick Darlene up, settle her in the apartment, and come back."

Tyce shoved back from the table. "I've got it covered. Pick-up time in twenty-five minutes." He winked at Melissa. "Shall we synchronize our watches?"

Melissa turned to Nancy. "Add cheeky to your list."

"You'll take all the fun out of this if that list gets much longer." Tyce picked up his empty food tray. "I have a couple things to pick up in my office. Then I'll head off to the senior center. Any last-minute instructions? Does Darlene have her key?"

For just a second he thought Melissa was going to change her mind and object to the plan. He could read the indecision on her face. Letting go was hard. Then she reached into her purse and pulled out a business card.

"Show this to Mary at the reception desk. Then she'll know it's okay for you to pick Darlene up."

He enclosed her hand in both of his as he reached for the card. "This will work out fine."

"I know. Thank you."

"Anytime." He couldn't think of a reason to hold her hand any longer. And if he did some of the students would begin to wonder.

In his office, Tyce grabbed some work he could take with him. The senior center was only a ten-minute drive, but he didn't want to be late. No telling what Darlene would do if someone weren't there to pick her up.

He pulled his car into a parking spot next to the center and got out. It was a brisk day, but the sun felt warm for the end of October. He glanced around as he entered the building. It was bright and cheery inside. Small tables were scattered around the room set up for playing games or snacking. Three men sat at a far table with dominoes spread on the table in front of them. They glanced up as Tyce entered, then returned to their game.

Four women sat around a table to the side finishing their lunch. Tyce smiled and they all smiled back.

"May I help you?" asked a pleasant woman behind the information counter.

"You must be Mary," Tyce said, fishing Melissa's card out of his pocket.

"Yes, I am." She looked surprised at his knowledge.

"Melissa said this would introduce me." He handed Mary the card. "I'm filling in for Melissa today in picking up Darlene Wilabee."

Mary's smile grew. "You must be Tyce. I've heard quite a lot about you."

"My reputation goes before me. But please don't hold it against me."

Mary chuckled. Then, glancing at the wall clock, she said, "The van hasn't arrived yet. Would you care for something to drink while you wait?"

"A cup of coffee would be fine."

Together they walked past the four women at the table and on to the counter where a big coffee urn sat. The sign next to the urn read "50 CENTS A CUP." Tyce reached into his pants pocket.

"Never mind." Mary patted his arm. "This cup's on me."

"Thank you."

The door to the center opened and a chattering group of senior citizens came in. Darlene was in the middle of the pack. She had her cane in one hand and the other tucked through the arm of a distinguished-looking gentleman. His gray hair waved back from his forehead, and his years had added a stoop to his shoulders.

Darlene has good taste. He noticed how solicitously the man led her into the room.

Tyce waited until everyone spread out a little and then walked over. "Hello, Darlene. Did you have a good outing this morning?"

Darlene looked a bit startled, but there was instant recognition in her eyes. "Tyce, what are you doing here?"

"I'm your substitute chauffeur."

"Good." She immediately switched to Tyce's arm.

Tyce waited for her to inquire about Melissa. But it seemed not even to have entered her mind.

"Before we head off let me introduce you to my friends." She turned to the gentleman, who still stood close by. "Dennis, this is Tyce."

"Nice to meet you, Tyce."

They shook hands, and then Darlene led Tyce over to the table where the four women were seated. "Ladies, I'd like you to meet my friend, Tyce."

"Hi, Tyce. I'm Madge. This is Alice." Madge pointed to the woman on her left, then to each of the others waiting to be introduced. "This is Elaine and that's Lila."

"Hello, ladies." Tyce could hardly contain his amusement. He felt like a trophy being shown off by its winner. Darlene led him around the room making sure everyone met him. Most of the time she didn't bother with names, and he suspected she didn't know them. He shook hands and smiled. "Hi—Hello—Nice to meet you." All the while he carried his Styrofoam cup of coffee hoping he wouldn't spill it on anyone.

"Guess that's everyone." Darlene looked around the room. "We can go now."

Tyce took a gulp of his lukewarm coffee. As he escorted

Darlene toward the door, he tossed the cup and remaining liquid into the trash. He tucked her safely into the passenger seat and got behind the wheel.

"I was thinking we could whip up some dinner before Melissa gets home. What would you like?" Tyce started the engine and pulled out onto the street.

"Are you sure we should?" Darlene sounded reluctant. "Melissa gets irked every time I suggest cooking."

"I'll take the blame if she gets upset." Tyce reached over and patted Darlene's hand. "I was thinking something simple. Maybe a stew. Would you help me shop?"

sixteen

All afternoon Melissa wondered if she'd done the right thing. *But what else could I do?* She argued the pros and cons. She berated herself for giving in too easily to the tempting offer of having Tyce pick up Darlene and stay with her while she helped the state examiner through his inspection of the records.

"That the last of the files?"

The examiner's question startled Melissa. Her mind had wandered to the apartment—wondering how Tyce and Darlene were getting along.

"Yes. That's the end of them."

"Very good. I'll send a copy of my report. You should get it in about two weeks."

When they had finished all the pleasantries, Melissa grabbed her coat and headed for home.

What if Mother has done something really strange? Like chase cats that aren't there. Or get in the shower with all her clothes on. She is probably capable of doing things I can't even imagine.

Melissa walked faster, hardly noticing the final roses of the season in the flower garden along the street.

Lord, don't let Mother have done something really embarrassing.

There I go, worrying about myself again. Not concerned whether she's safe—just so I'm not embarrassed.

Forgive me, Lord. Melissa took a deep breath, slowed her pace, and continued to talk to her heavenly Father. By the time she reached the apartment, she felt relaxed. She slid the key into the lock and turned the handle. A hearty aroma greeted her as she shoved open the door.

"Hi. How did your afternoon go?" Tyce said. "Examiner get through?"

"Yes, it went smoothly." Melissa tipped her head slightly and inhaled the smell coming from the kitchen. "What's cooking?"

"Ah. That would be supper."

"You've cooked supper?" The incredible possibility sent her voice up the scale.

"Well, I'm not just a pretty face."

Melissa grinned then giggled. Handsome, strong, rugged could all describe Tyce. But pretty? Never!

"I told Darlene I'd take the blame if you got mad at us for messing around in your kitchen."

"Where is Mother?"

"She hasn't come out of the bedroom since she went in to take a nap. Maybe we should check and see if she's all right."

Melissa nodded and headed to the bedroom. Tyce trailed along behind.

"I guess I should have been checking up on her." Tyce sounded so contrite Melissa felt guilty.

"No, no. Unless I hear noises in there, I don't bother her."

"What kind of noises?"

The only person who knew about the invisible cat breaking in, besides Melissa and Darlene, was the 911 operator. Melissa planned on keeping it that way.

"You know. If she should yell or it sounds like something falling."

Melissa opened the door and peeked in, then closed it gently. "Still sleeping."

Tyce returned to the papers spread over the table. "I didn't realize how many interruptions I have at school. This has been nice to work undisturbed." As though Melissa's words had finally sunk in, he asked, "Does she often yell in her sleep?"

"No, I just used that as an example." Melissa wasn't sure what to do next. She'd like to get out of her work clothes and slip into jeans. But that meant getting clothes out of the drawers behind the chair and changing in the bathroom. She'd just wait. When did he plan on leaving? She couldn't even suggest he leave before he'd had supper. That would be the height of ungratefulness, since he'd made the stew.

"Making any headway in locating your father?"

"There are a couple of possibilities."

"Really!"

His enthusiasm softened Melissa's resolve to find her father on her own. What would it hurt to discuss it with Tyce? "I received an interesting call from Gilbert."

"He's helping you locate your father?"

Melissa heard the surprise and hurt in Tyce's voice before he quickly covered it with, "That's nice of him."

"Gilbert has volunteered his parents' help."

"They know something about locating lost people?"

Melissa spent the next few minutes repeating Gilbert's phone message. "They might have helpful information."

"I'd say it was worth looking into. At least it would give you a new perspective on your father."

"Yes. I'd like to hear about him from someone who liked him."

"You said you had two possibilities?"

"I looked up a company in the phone book. Let me get the paper." She went to her desk and pulled out a sheet of typing paper. "It says they have offices and agents nationwide, low-cost services, all calls confidential. They specialize in deadbeat parents, locating lost heirs and loved ones."

"Have you given them a call?"

"No." Melissa slowly shook her head. "I keep thinking I can find him on my own. I haven't even tried yet. The least I can do is try."

"And while you're tracking down clues, you'll be learning more about your father."

"Right." Melissa sat down in the chair next to Tyce. Suddenly, she was eager to share her hopes and dreams. She leaned toward him. "This is the most exciting thing that has happened to me. I feel like I've been given a present. Something so special it takes my breath away. At times I almost pinch myself to see if I'm awake and not dreaming."

"Are you heading for Turner again this weekend?"

"No. I think that might be too soon for Mother."

"Too bad you can't go without her. I'm sure people will be much more willing to talk if they don't feel inhibited by her presence."

"To do that I'll have to wait until Beverly gets back."

"Not necessarily."

Melissa looked inquiringly at Tyce then shook her head. "I know what you're going to say. And no, you're not coming over here and taking charge for a whole weekend."

"Give me one good reason why not. And I mean good."

"This isn't your problem."

"As a friend, I'm making it my problem. You'll have to do better than that."

Melissa opened her mouth then snapped it shut. She was drawing a blank. She tried again, "I. . ."

Tyce gave her a triumphant look. "It will work out. We have a week to put the plan together."

A small noise came from the bedroom. "Sounds like Mother's up."

"I'll clear my stuff off the table so we can eat."

Darlene shuffle-thumped her way down the hall. "Oh, we have company."

"Yes, Mother. Tyce is joining us for supper. Did you enjoy your trip today?"

"Trip?"

"I think you went with the seniors to the Frye Art Museum and then had lunch out."

"No."

Melissa caught herself before she began arguing. "I'll have supper on in a jiffy. Take a seat." On the way to the kitchen, she told herself it didn't matter that Darlene couldn't remember.

Pretend she's someone else's mother. Isn't that Tyce's solution?

Isn't it sad that Mrs. Brown is failing so fast? Her imaginary dialogue surprised her. That was exactly what she would say if Darlene belonged to someone else. And having said it, she would go about her business with no further thought about how it affected Mrs. Brown's daughter.

She wouldn't blame Mrs. Brown's daughter for her mother's condition. She probably wouldn't even realize how embarrassed Daughter Brown felt.

When I quit worrying about what people are thinking about me, I'll realize they aren't thinking of me at all.

"Can I help you with anything?" Tyce stood just inside the kitchen.

"Do you have special instructions for serving your stew?"

"It's just stew."

"Shall we have crackers and cheese with it?"

"That sounds good."

When everything was on the table, Melissa said grace and took a tentative bite. "This is marvelous!"

"Don't sound so surprised." Tyce grinned at her embarrassment. "I'm a multitalented person."

"I didn't mean for that to sound so negative. But my stews never taste this good. What's your secret?"

Tyce's eyes twinkled, and he winked at Darlene. "We'll never tell, will we?"

Melissa watched her mother join in the conspiracy by shaking her head and doing the childlike gesture of zipping her mouth.

Dear Mrs. Brown—I wonder why we could never have a relationship like that? Melissa felt the squeezing pressure in her chest that always came before a crying jag. *Don't feel sorry for yourself, Daughter Brown. Mrs. Brown may have wondered the same thing.*

Watch Tyce. Watch closely. He seems to be able to relate. Maybe you can learn something. Join in.

"All right, you two. If you won't tell me the secret, Tyce will just have to come over and fix it for us again."

"You heard her, Darlene. I now have an official invitation to come back."

Darlene nodded emphatically. "You come back anytime. No matter what Melissa says. She doesn't know what's good for her."

"Thank you. It's always nice to be wanted." Tyce reached for the pot of stew. "I'm going to have another helping. May I serve you some more?"

Darlene shook her head, covering her bowl with her hand. "One is enough for me."

"Melissa?"

"Yes, please."

"You know, Tyce," Darlene said, leaning toward him and lowering her voice, "Melissa has never been a good cook. I can remember trying to teach her when she was little. I'd put those cute little aprons on Beverly and Melissa and try to show them how to bake cookies. Melissa was hopeless. Of course, she was always such a gangly child. So tall for her age."

Daughter Brown is about to sustain a major humiliation. But will anyone remember a week from now? No. So forget it.

Tyce leaned closer to Darlene. "She sure did grow out of the gangly stage. But since she's sitting right here, maybe we should stop talking about her."

The thought seemed to surprise Darlene. She looked at Melissa as if astonished to find her sitting across the table.

Melissa concentrated on eating her stew. She welcomed the lull that settled over the table.

Hardly tasting the last bite of stew, her mind took up the possibility of driving to Turner for the weekend. It did seem Tyce and Darlene got along splendidly. He knew the right words to say. He certainly could be trusted with her well-being. There didn't seem to be any reason not to accept his offer. Except! The big except. It would make her indebted to him.

She'd be relying on him. She'd be trusting him. And years ago she'd vowed never to put herself in that position again. The one man in her life hadn't been trustworthy.

But it wasn't true. She'd lived with a lie all her life. Daddy wasn't the one to blame. Her mother had been the liar.

"Melissa, are you all right?" Tyce reached out and covered her hand with his. "You look stressed."

"I'm all right." Everything's all right, she wanted to shout. It's all right to trust Tyce.

"Good. I think I better be getting on my way." He picked up his bowl and silverware and headed to the kitchen.

"Don't bother with that," Melissa said, taking the dishes from him. "The least I can do is clean up after you prepared the meal. And it was an excellent meal."

Tyce grinned. "Thanks. See you tomorrow then."

She closed the door behind Tyce and leaned against the cool wood.

"When are you going to get your act together and marry that guy?" Darlene scowled from the rocking chair where she'd taken up residence.

Melissa just smiled. *Mrs. Brown is at it again.*

"Have you heard any more from Beverly?" Darlene switched the conversation. "She should be home by now."

"Not a word. Nothing since she called and told you they were staying another three weeks in England."

"The least she could do is drop us a postcard."

"Would be nice to know how things are going," Melissa agreed.

Petey ruffled his feathers, swung upside down from his perch, and gave a squawk.

"Show off," Darlene said.

"Why don't you give Petey to your neighbor girl? What's her name?"

"Why would I give Petey away to anyone?" Darlene appeared truly bewildered.

"Maybe because you don't like him."

"Who says I don't like him?"

"You don't take care of him."

"Now why should I take care of the bird when I have you and Beverly to do it for me?"

Melissa realized the conversation was going nowhere. "You're absolutely right."

She wondered about mentioning the return trip to Turner. No, plans weren't set in place yet. And as she thought about the weekend, her mind was full of Tyce.

He must sincerely care about me to make an offer to stay with Darlene. What other man would go out of his way like that to help. Gilbert! Poor Gilbert, why can't he find a girl who returns his affection? Maybe I should wait until after the first of the year to go speak to Mr. and Mrs. Reese. Then she wouldn't be subjecting Gilbert to her presence again. *But I don't want to wait. You'd think a month or two wouldn't make a difference after waiting twenty-five years, but it does.*

"Have you read your father's letters?"

Darlene's question shocked Melissa. Darlene had made no reference to the letters or even to the trip to Turner since their return.

"Yes, Mother. I've read them." There were questions she'd love to have answered. But she didn't want to quarrel with Darlene, so she kept her reply short.

"I suppose you're going to try and find him." Darlene's voice was so even and reasonable Melissa's hopes lifted.

"I would like to find him."

"What do you hope to accomplish by finding him?"

"To start, I'd like to tell him I don't hate him anymore. And ask his forgiveness."

Darlene made an inarticulate sound. Melissa couldn't decipher its meaning.

"It's important to me that he knows I didn't refuse his letters and gifts."

Darlene looked up sharply from the thread her fingers had been worrying on the arm of the rocker.

Melissa held her breath. Had she been wrong to mention the gifts?

"Well, it's too late for all that now."

"It's never too late to mend fences and build bridges."

"It is if he's dead."

seventeen

"Father's dead?" Melissa's mind refused the information. "My father is dead?"

"I don't know." Darlene rocked back and forth. "He could be, you know. He hasn't been in touch for years."

Was her mother being deliberately cruel?

"I'd better clean up in the kitchen." Melissa escaped before she said something she'd regret later. She took her time, although it was obvious Tyce had cleaned up after himself. There were only the supper dishes to rinse and put into the dishwasher. She puttered around, rearranging some spice jars in the cupboard, wiping down shelves, and giving the kitchen counter a polish.

She heard Darlene get up and head for the bedroom. With irritation still gnawing at her, she didn't call good night.

❧

"I hear your search for your father is under way." Nancy beamed as she came into Melissa's office. "This is so exciting."

"I see you and Tyce have been comparing notes again." She didn't know why the thought upset her.

"Oh, Melissa, I hope you don't mind. Just tell me to mind my own business if this is a covert operation." Nancy hardly paused before adding, "But I have this marvelous idea."

Melissa waited for Nancy to continue. She was standing expectantly in front of the desk leaning forward in anticipation.

"And?" Melissa prompted.

As though announcing a major coup, Nancy said, "I'll keep Darlene for the weekend, and you and Tyce can go to Turner together."

Melissa's mouth dropped open. She snapped it shut and

shook her head. "Why would you think Tyce was coming to Turner with me?"

"I figure you could learn disturbing or—" She paused for effect. "Shocking information. You shouldn't be alone at a time like this."

"You think there could be something more shocking than finding I've lived with a lie for twenty-five years? I really think there won't be many more surprises. At least not any I can't deal with." Could there be? She wondered. When Melissa's mind stopped wandering, Nancy was still standing in front of her.

Melissa got up and came around the desk. She gathered Nancy in a hug. "I do appreciate your offer. Truly, I do."

"Here comes the big but."

Melissa laughed. "I can hardly ask Tyce to go to Turner with me. I know he drove us down last weekend, but there is a limit."

Now it was Nancy's turn to laugh. "You don't have to ask. We already discussed it, and he's eager to go."

This time Melissa couldn't even think of a retort. She simply backed away and stared at her friend as though the whole world were in league against her.

Nancy chattered on while Melissa's mind reeled.

"We can do this one of two ways. I can come stay at your apartment or, better yet, Darlene can come stay with me. I have two bedrooms, you know."

"Do I have any say in this?" Melissa finally interrupted.

"Of course you do." Nancy closed the gap between them and whispered, "Say yes."

≈

It wasn't until noon that she saw Tyce. He came into the cafeteria wearing light gray slacks and a charcoal pullover. Her heart skipped a beat at the sight of him. He was walking with one of the older professors, a man slightly stooped with a fringe of gray hair. The contrast made Tyce seem bigger than life. Any objections she'd raised to having him accompany her to Turner disappeared at the sight of him.

She was being foolish to fight this attraction she felt for him. The lies of the past shouldn't be allowed to discolor the future. Now was the time to start fresh, to build a new life on the truth. And part of that truth was she'd fallen in love with Tyce Nelson.

"May I join you?" Tyce stood at her elbow holding his tray.

"Please do." A sense of peace settled over Melissa. She'd quit fighting. The surprise was how easy it was to let go. She could feel a smile bubbling up from inside her.

"You're looking happy." Tyce looked deeply into her eyes. "Something special happen?"

Her first instinct was to say, Someone special happened. But she decided to hang onto her secret awhile longer.

"The possibility of finding my father has changed my whole outlook on life."

"I'm glad you're feeling good about this." Tyce cut off a bite of sliced ham on his plate and popped it into his mouth.

Melissa could tell he wasn't finished with his thought. "You're hoping I'm not letting circumstances dictate my happiness. Am I right?"

"You read my mind," Tyce said.

"I hadn't realized how much my father's leaving affected the rest of my life. Before all this came to light, I would have said I was a happy person. But deep inside me was a root of bitterness."

"What are you doing about it?"

Melissa pushed the tomato around in her salad. Count on Tyce not to let her off the hook. "A couple of things are helping."

She faced him and grinned. "For one thing, Darlene has become Mrs. Brown."

"You lost me." Tyce's brow furrowed.

"Remember? It's easier to deal with someone else's parent.

A very wise man told me that once. So, Mrs. Brown's daughter will have to deal with her mother's erratic behavior."

Tyce's laugh made heads turn in the cafeteria. "Good for you. Does it work?"

"Pretty well."

"You say there are a couple things. What else?"

"I've decided to stop fighting my friends and accept all the help I can get." She took a bite of the chocolate chip cookie she'd picked for dessert. It was still fresh enough from the oven to melt in her mouth. "That's a warning, by the way. You have one hour to renege on any offer you've made, and after that you're stuck."

Tyce glanced at his watch. "Only one hour?"

❧

"I'm still a bit uneasy about leaving Nancy to cope with Darlene." Melissa sat in the passenger seat of Tyce's car. They'd gotten through downtown Seattle traffic without a glitch.

"Nancy's the most sensible person I know. They'll do fine. It's a good thing you told her about the invisible cat episode. The fewer surprises, the better."

Melissa nodded.

It would be after ten before they arrived in Turner so Melissa had made an appointment to see Mr. and Mrs. Reese at eleven Saturday morning. She could feel butterflies every time she thought about it.

The butterflies had grown to hummingbirds by Saturday morning when Tyce drove over from the motel to Beverly's house to pick up Melissa and take her out to breakfast.

"I don't think I can eat a thing." Melissa placed a hand on her stomach to see if it would help quiet the jitters. "I'm so excited, I'm about to explode."

"Don't get yourself on such a high there's no place to go but down."

Melissa managed to eat a piece of toast and a few bites of

scrambled eggs at the restaurant. Then she sat and watched Tyce polish off a large stack with eggs and sausage.

"Sorry to keep you waiting," he apologized as he drained the last of his coffee.

"I wouldn't want you fainting from hunger before lunchtime. Besides, we still have an hour before my appointment with the Reeses."

"What do you want to do in the meantime? Anything else you want to look for at your mother's place?"

"I don't think so."

"How about showing me the places you remember from your childhood?"

"Yes. I know just the place."

They parked a short distance from Mill Creek, which meandered through the heart of town. Melissa led him to the spot on the bank where she'd spent time with her father.

"Remember the shoebox we found?" She spread a car robe on the ground and sat down, patting the spot beside her for Tyce to join her. "I don't know how many times we came here. And I don't ever remember Beverly being with us. Just Daddy and me."

"It's nice to have good memories."

"Unfortunately, the lies spoiled them." She recounted the day she broke the willow fishing pole. They sat in silence watching minnows in the shallows until it was time to go for her interview.

Gilbert threw open the door as they walked up the path. "Hi, guys."

Melissa hadn't let the Reeses know she was bringing Tyce. Gilbert's hearty welcome relieved her mind.

"Hi. How's it going?" Tyce gave Gilbert a friendly handshake.

"Good. Good. Getting ready to head south to look for an apartment. I have a couple weeks' vacation coming and thought I'd put them to good use." He turned to Melissa. "Come on in;

the folks are anxious to talk with you."

The Reeses were a quaint couple. Gilbert had gotten his tall thin frame from his father. The red hair came from his mother. She was as short and heavy as he was tall and thin. They welcomed Melissa and Tyce in a boisterous manner.

"Come in. Come in." Repeating oneself seemed to run in the family.

"What smells so good?" Tyce asked as they entered.

"That's hot cider." Mrs. Reese beamed. "It's getting close enough to Thanksgiving to get out the cider. Always say it goes with the holidays. It'll be ready in a minute or two. Just sit down and make yourselves at home."

"Thank you." Melissa perched on a kitchen chair that had been brought into the living room.

"Oh, my dear. You don't want to sit there. The sofa's much more comfortable."

Melissa didn't argue, although she could tell the sagging piece of furniture referred to as the sofa would be anything but comfortable.

"Excuse me now, and I'll bring in the cider. Gilbert, you come and help me carry the tray."

Melissa glanced around the room. She'd never been in Gilbert's house as a kid. But she was sure the decor hadn't changed in all this time. Old-fashioned plaques dotted the walls. One caught her eye just above an old upright piano: JESUS NEVER FAILS. The words were written in a fancy script, and a pair of robins perched in one corner on a blooming apple tree branch. She was still looking at it when Gilbert and his mother returned.

"Now let's get on with why you're here," Mrs. Reese said, setting a cup of steaming cider in front of Melissa on the wobbly coffee table. "I've known your mother since we were in grade school together. But your dad didn't come until after we graduated from high school. The minute he set eyes on Darlene, the rest of us girls didn't have a chance."

"Lucky for me." Mr. Reese had perched on the arm of the overstuffed chair Mrs. Reese occupied, and he nudged her with his elbow as he spoke.

"Oh, you." She gave him a playful slap.

They're in love still. It seemed incongruous that she was here to talk to the Reeses about her parents, who hadn't stayed together long enough to celebrate a tenth anniversary. And it was probable their love had died long before that.

What would it have been like to be raised in a loving home like this? How would she be different now? Melissa realized she'd gone off into her own little world when she heard Tyce.

"Did you go to their wedding?" he asked.

"Oh my, yes. Your mother made a beautiful bride, and Frank was so handsome. I think half the town turned out for their wedding."

"Did they seem happy?" The question asked itself before Melissa could stop it.

Melissa read the sympathy in Mrs. Reese's eyes.

"I think your mother was as happy as I've ever seen her."

It was an evasive answer, and Melissa pushed on. "Tell me about my father."

Mr. Reese cleared his throat and stared at a spot in the far corner of the ceiling.

"Your father was a good man. Well liked by everyone in town. Even though he was a newcomer, he could call you by name when you passed on the street. We all felt kinda sorry for him."

"Now don't go telling her that kind of stuff," Mrs. Reese admonished.

"It's all right," Melissa hastened to say.

"I think she's come looking for the truth." He bristled a little and gave his wife a no-nonsense look. "And I think she deserves to hear it."

She nodded but didn't look too happy with the decision.

"Your mother wasn't the easiest person to live with."

Melissa laughed. "She still isn't." That seemed to break the tension that had settled over the room. "Don't be afraid to hurt my feelings. Like you said, I'm just looking for the truth."

"He loved your mother. He'd do anything to keep your mother happy. Guess that's why the town was so surprised when he dug in his heels and fought for custody of you during the divorce. Seems like when he lost the battle he just gave up. Moved away—to California, I think."

"Do you know if he was originally from California?" Melissa waited for the answer while the butterflies wheeled in her stomach.

"Now let me see." Mr. Reese looked at his wife. "Don't reckon I remember."

"I remember all right." Mrs. Reese smiled as though recalling something pleasant. "Good-looking city fellow comes to town. I bet every girl in town could tell you where he was from. Los Angeles. Yes, indeed."

Melissa listened spellbound as a picture from The Music Man formed in her mind. "Was he a salesman?"

"Oh, no, Dearie. Your father came here as assistant to the vice president of the bank."

"A banker? I never knew that."

"What did your mother tell you he did?" Mr. Reese leaned forward scowling.

"Mother never talked about him."

"Tsk, tsk." The sound of pity came from Mrs. Reese as she shook her head.

They talked for two hours. Melissa savored every word about her father.

"There's one other thing might help locate him," Mr. Reese said as they shook hands good-bye. "I just remembered he joined the Grange. You know, Darlene's folks owned that big farm, and they were stanch Grangers. If he still belongs, or has Grange Insurance you might track him that way."

Back at Beverly's house, Melissa curled up in the corner of the couch with her notebook, making notes of everything she'd learned.

Tyce pulled out a current bestseller, and they sat in silence.

It struck Melissa that they were acting like an old married couple. Comfortable in each other's company, they didn't need small talk. However, his presence had every nerve ending on alert. Even as she wrote about her father, her mind kept coming back to the man across the room.

She looked up to study his head bowed over the book. His good looks were rugged, the nose a bit too broad for perfection. He completely filled the reclining chair he'd chosen. He was tilted back just enough to make lots of lap room. She felt the surge of heat rise as she realized where her thoughts were taking her. Just then he looked up.

The flame rose to her cheeks, and she dropped her gaze back to the notebook. She wrote until she couldn't recall another detail she hadn't recorded. Sometimes she tried to write the dialogue verbatim, to catch the flavor of the Reeses' comments. On the page with pertinent information for finding her father, she added his occupation and membership in the Grange.

"We skipped lunch." Tyce's voice broke the stillness. "Would you like an early supper?"

"Sounds good. I think my appetite is back. I'll get ready." She brushed her hair and applied a new coat of lipstick.

Tyce was standing by the door holding her coat when she came back downstairs. She slid into the coat, and he lifted her hair away from the collar. As he did his hand brushed the nape of her neck. She felt the tingle all the way to her toes.

eighteen

Tyce slammed the book shut. Unfortunately, a book on managing your small business couldn't compete with thoughts of Melissa.

Two days had passed since he and Melissa returned from Turner. It had taken a supreme act of will not to declare his love to Melissa that last evening. She'd been radiant. Learning about her father had acted like a spring tonic. He could see it in her eyes and hear it in her laughter.

On the drive home, they'd discussed where to begin on the actual search for her father. As they talked she'd made a list. Now it was up to her to follow through. There didn't seem to be much else he could do to help.

Absently, he rubbed the back of his hand—the place that had made contact with her neck. It had been an accidental touching, and the electricity of it sent a shock through him he wasn't expecting. Even now he could replay the sensations.

The ringing phone jerked him back to the present.

"Hello."

"Tyce." Melissa's frantic voice came over the wire. "Mother's missing."

"Slow down. Give it to me from the top."

"Mother lay down for a nap after I picked her up at the center. Since she was all settled, I decided to run to the store."

"Hang on. I'll be there in two minutes." He grabbed his jacket, pocketed his keys, and sprinted across the parking lot. All the while he prayed Darlene was okay. Melissa didn't need this frustration now.

Melissa was waiting for him at the outside door. "I walked all around the complex before calling you, but I can't find her."

"Time to call out the troops."

"Oh, Tyce. I feel so. . ."

"Hey. Mrs. Brown has gone missing, and we're the ones who need to do something about it." He reached for her arm. "Come on. Let's make some phone calls."

Melissa almost managed a smile, but Tyce could see it went no deeper than the curve of her lip.

Back in her apartment, Tyce picked up the school directory beside the phone. He dialed Nancy and then one of the boys at the dorm. "Help's on the way," he reported when he hung up.

"I left a note on the table saying I'd be right back. I guess I was gone a half hour. But she always takes a longer nap than that."

"It's okay." Melissa looked so pitiful, Tyce gathered her into his arms. She relaxed against him and rested her head on his shoulder.

"Remind me to thank Darlene for taking off," he whispered against her hair.

As he intended, it was just what Melissa needed. She straightened and with a genuine smile asked, "Shall I call the police?"

"It wouldn't hurt."

When an hour had passed and there was still no sign of Darlene, Tyce began to worry. All the local stores and restaurants had been searched by the students. Because of her days of working in the school offices the students were familiar with Darlene, so the possibility of missing her was slim. If she'd gotten farther than the surrounding blocks, it meant someone had picked her up and given her a ride.

The sun slid behind the Olympic Mountains as Tyce picked up the phone. He dialed the first cab company in the phone book, then made his way down the list as each call proved unproductive.

"She didn't go by cab," he announced, hanging up again. "Suppose she would take a bus?"

"I don't know." There was no smile left—only a worried pucker between her eyebrows. "She didn't ride buses in Turner."

Melissa grabbed the phone on the first ring. "Hello. Hi, Nancy. Any news?"

Tyce could tell there had been no success from the droop of Melissa's shoulders as she listened to Nancy.

"Thanks." Melissa hung up. "What do I do now? I can't expect the students to continue looking. And I can't stand this waiting here."

"Okay. Call Nancy back. Ask her to come and sit by the phone, and we'll go out looking."

Being able to take action brought the spark back to Melissa's eyes. She placed the call then gathered her coat and gloves. "I wonder what mother was wearing?" She went to the bedroom and did a quick search. "Her coat's gone. That's a good sign."

It was twelve minutes before Nancy rang the bell. When she came in, she gave Melissa a big hug. "We're going to find her." She turned to Tyce. "Any idea where you're going to look?"

He shook his head.

Melissa and Tyce left the apartment and headed toward his car. As they came down the sidewalk, a city bus pulled up to the curb. He dashed toward the bus.

"Where are you going?" Melissa called after him.

He reached the bus just as one passenger disembarked.

"Excuse me." He climbed two steps into the bus. "We're looking for a missing person and think she may have caught a bus here between four-thirty and five. Is there any way I can get hold of the driver of that bus to see where she got off?"

The driver gave him a suspicious look. "We can't give out that kind of information to just anyone."

"You're right. I'll get Sergeant Lewis to contact the bus company. Sorry to hold you up." Tyce stepped out, and Melissa was there waiting.

"What was that all about?"

"If Darlene took a bus, the company might be able to tell

the police where she got off." Tyce pulled out his cell phone and called the sergeant's number. He had a hunch that Darlene was about to be found.

❧

"I can't believe she actually got on a bus." Melissa sat beside Tyce as they drove to the Northgate bus station. It didn't take the police long to discover Darlene had ridden the bus to the station. When she didn't get off, the driver had gone to the back of the bus to check on her.

Melissa hadn't gotten all the details over the phone, but she could imagine the scenario: A befuddled old woman gets on the bus then doesn't know where she's going or even where she wants to go.

"You know, we're lucky she didn't change buses and end up in Everett or Marysville."

"Is that supposed to be encouraging?" Melissa's nerves made her snap at Tyce. Then she shook her head. "It's not just this. It's the rest of her life. What am I going to do? I can't leave her alone a minute." Melissa choked back a sob. "Forgive me. I'm feeling sorry for myself again."

"When Beverly gets back, you'll have to make a plan. I don't think either of you can handle Darlene without help."

"There're four more weeks before Beverly comes back. Right now that sounds like forever. I wish I knew what to do in the meantime."

Tyce pulled into the bus terminal. "Here we are." A police car sat near the entrance. Tyce and Melissa got out and approached the car.

Sergeant Lewis stepped out. Melissa could see Darlene sitting in the rear of the car.

"What's it been? Two weeks since she took off last time?" the sergeant asked.

Good grief. My mother has some kind of police record. Melissa schooled her expression to hide her dismay. "Thank you. It was such a relief to know you'd found Mother."

Sergeant Lewis opened the back door for Darlene.

"It's about time you got here," Darlene said as she climbed out of the police car.

"My fault," Tyce said.

Darlene looked around with a bewildered gaze. "Where's Beverly?"

"She couldn't make it. But Melissa and I came." Tyce pulled Melissa close to him and squeezed her shoulder.

Melissa couldn't take her eyes off her mother. Her hair looked like she'd just gotten out of bed. She had her coat on, all right, but it gapped open in front disclosing a white slip.

"It's getting chilly out here," Tyce said and removed his arm from Melissa's shoulder. "Let's head home."

The second his arm was gone Melissa felt bereft.

Tyce opened the front passenger door and helped Darlene in.

Twice on the way home Darlene asked, "Where's Beverly?"

Melissa sat in the back and listened as Tyce patiently replied, "She couldn't make it."

Why can't Mother remember a simple thing like why Beverly isn't here? Melissa felt frustration gnawing at her insides.

Reaching the apartment, Melissa hurried Darlene into the bedroom. Maybe Tyce hadn't noticed she was only wearing a slip under her coat. It had been a shock to see her mother out in public so disheveled. Never in her right mind would Darlene leave the apartment without combing her hair.

The slow realization that her mother had no control over this illness sank into Melissa's heart. All her anger and frustration, her whys and how comes, could not slow the progress of dementia.

When Darlene was tucked in bed, Melissa turned out the light and returned to the living room. For a split second she was startled to see Tyce sitting on the sofa.

"I didn't know you were still here."

"I won't stay long. Just wanted to make sure everything was all right."

"All right?" Melissa shook her head. "Mother's never going to be all right again."

"There is some peace in knowing Darlene won't remember much of tonight. Come, sit down." He patted the sofa beside him. "You're the one I'm concerned about."

"I'm fine."

Tyce gazed at Melissa without saying anything until she finally shrugged. "Okay. I'm not fine."

He picked up one of Melissa's hands and stroked the back of it with his thumb. "You have a plate full to overflowing. Between your sister, mother, and father you are shouldering more than your share of the load." He paused with a grin. "I think I just mixed my metaphors. But you get the picture."

Melissa looked into his smiling eyes. Just having him beside her was a comfort. Once her family life straightened out, she'd think about where this relationship might lead.

He'd relaxed against the sofa in a way indicating he had no intention of leaving soon. She accepted his decision and swiveled around until she was leaning comfortably against his shoulder.

"I've had something on my mind for awhile," he said, releasing her hand and putting his right arm around her. "I've hesitated to mention it since you have a few other things to think about."

Melissa closed her eyes. *This must be how a rag doll feels. If he doesn't say what he has to say and leave soon, I'll fall asleep right here on his shoulder.*

"In case you haven't guessed, I love you."

That's nice. Hearing his voice made her all warm and fuzzy inside. He sounded a long way off.

"Melissa."

She thought she heard her name.

"Melissa. Are you awake?"

"Hmm."

"I'm leaving now. You need your rest."

"Okay." The one word seemed to take her last bit of strength. She struggled to open her eyes. There was something she should say.

"Good night."

She felt a blanket being tucked around her shoulders as she slid into a reclining position.

❧

Melissa awoke to the realization that she was very cold. She felt for a corner of the blanket to pull up around her neck, but her fingers groped in vain. She started to roll over and nearly fell off the sofa. She sat up with a start.

A night-light in the hall revealed she was fully dressed. A blanket lay on the floor beside the sofa. Slowly memory returned. Darlene had taken off again. Fortunately, with Tyce's help they'd found her. Tyce! They'd been sitting on this sofa. She'd evidently fallen asleep.

Then the words came back. "I love you." Had she dreamed it? What had she replied?

Now she was wide awake. *Did I dream the whole thing?* she asked herself again. *And how do I find out? I can't walk up and say, "Excuse me, Tyce. Did you say you loved me last night?"*

She got up and headed to the bedroom. While she was up she'd check on her mother. Her humiliation at finding her mother half dressed washed over her again. It was going to be hard to credit this episode to Mrs. Brown.

The next morning, after dropping Darlene at the senior center, Melissa headed to the college. If she were walking, she'd be dragging her heels. She knew what had caused her to crash last night. Stress had finally caught up with her. But fatigue didn't seem to be a very good reason for falling asleep while Tyce declared his love. She amended the thought. If he declared his love.

"What a mess!"

nineteen

Melissa pulled into the school parking lot and bowed her head on the steering wheel. "Lord." Her mind ran around in circles. What should she pray for? "Lord, I just give it all to You. I haven't the slightest idea how to handle any of the things going on in my life right now. Show me, Lord. Let the answers be so obvious even I can't miss them. In the precious name of Jesus, amen."

Melissa's office door stood open as she came down the hall. She peeked around the corner to see Nancy sitting in her chair.

"There you are!" Nancy jumped up and came around the desk. "I couldn't wait to talk to you this morning."

The last thing Melissa wanted was a rehash of Darlene's latest episode. But she put a smile on her face anyway. "What's up?"

"Last night I received a phone call from my nephew, Neal. I'm not sure if you've ever met him. He's my brother Stanley's boy."

Melissa took off her coat and hung it on the coat stand behind the door. She let out a sigh of relief that Nancy had something on her mind besides Darlene.

"Neal's a freshman at the U of W and really into computers. Anyway, we got around to talking about what I've been doing, and I mentioned the weekend with Darlene."

Melissa chuckled. It seemed everything came back to Darlene. Then she remembered her prayer. If God was going to show her what to do, she'd better pay attention to everything going on around her. Even Nancy's chatter.

"I'm so glad you can still laugh after last night," Nancy said.

"I worry about you."

"Thanks for caring. I'll make it." Melissa didn't know how, but she'd left it in God's hands, and she wasn't going to snatch it back. "What did you want to tell me about Neal?"

"When I mentioned you'd gone to Turner to find out about your father, Neal asked why you didn't locate him on the Internet."

"I don't understand."

"I didn't either. I mean, I can type on a computer and do E-mail, but I'm not into all the Web business."

Melissa nodded. Although she had a computer at home, after spending all day working on one in the office, it didn't hold much appeal in the evening. She'd rather curl up with a book. She hadn't even had a chance to do that in the last four weeks.

"What does the Internet have to do with my father?"

"There's this on-line phone book thing. You type in the Web address and hit—let me find the words—here it is." She glanced at a piece of paper. "People search. You type in the name you're looking for and the state they're in, and it gives you their phone number."

Tyce walked in the door as Nancy finished her explanation.

"Hey, that's a good idea. Let's do it."

"I'll do it first thing when I get home this evening."

"No, do it now," Tyce urged.

"I don't like to use the school computer for personal stuff."

"This is the exception to the rule," Nancy said.

Melissa knew she'd have trouble concentrating on work until she found out what information the computer could give her. And she'd asked God for solutions only minutes ago. Could this be part of the answer already?

"Come on." Nancy gave Melissa a push toward her computer.

"Okay. What was the address again?" A few strokes of the keys brought the menu up. As she typed in her father's name, Franklin Wilabee, Melissa felt the excited tempo of her heartbeat. She hit the search button.

"Look," Nancy said, leaning over Melissa's shoulder. "Six Franklin Wilabees in California. Which one is your father?"

"I guess the only way to find out is to call."

"This is so exciting."

Melissa hit "print screen" and waited until the printer spit the page out.

"Which one are you going to call first?"

"I'll think about it."

"You're not going to call now?"

Nancy's crestfallen look made Tyce and Melissa laugh.

"No. I'm not going to make long-distance calls on the school phone."

"Of course. You're right. But how can you stand to wait?"

"Actually I'd like awhile to think about what I'm going to say."

"Not to be a wet blanket," Tyce said. "But there is always the possibility that none of these is the right Franklin Wilabee. Just keep this all in perspective."

"I just feel Melissa's on the right track," Nancy said, heading for the door. "Would you give me a call tonight? I don't think I could stand to wait until tomorrow. After all, it was my suggestion."

Melissa read down the computer printout. Could this be the end of her search? It seemed too easy.

"I better get back to my office."

Melissa looked up as Tyce spoke. His mouth was curved up at the corners in a warm smile. This time her racing heart had nothing to do with a computer search. His eyes told her all sorts of things she hardly dared to translate into words.

"See you at lunch," Melissa managed to say. Her chest felt heavy, and at the same time she had a distinct floating sensation.

❧

The afternoon flew by. To Melissa's surprise, she could concentrate on her work. She found herself humming several times. The words to an old familiar hymn rang through her mind. *"Praise to the Lord, the Almighty, the King of creation."* Ever since she'd made a deliberate effort to turn her problems over to God this morning, things had been going splendidly.

She filed away the last student folder, and that left one piece of paper on her desk—the one containing the list of California phone numbers.

"Hi." Tyce stood in the open doorway. "Do you need some time alone this evening?"

Melissa frowned at the strange question. "What do you mean?"

"Just that when you make your phone calls, maybe you'd be more comfortable if Darlene wasn't sitting in the same room."

"That's probably true, but there's really only one room besides the bedroom in my apartment. And, anyway, Mother knows I'm trying to get in touch with my father."

"What if I invite her to my place for supper? That will give you a bit of breathing space."

Melissa's eyes widened. "You are too good to be believed."

"I take it that's a yes." Tyce slouched against the doorframe. "I'll give you a half hour to pick Darlene up and get back to the apartment. Then I'll call and invite her. Would six o'clock be a good time to eat?"

"It would be perfect."

He gave her his conspiratorial wink as he straightened up. "See you later."

This day couldn't get any better, Melissa thought as she pulled into the senior center. She spotted Darlene as soon as she walked in the door.

Melissa and Darlene had been in the apartment ten minutes when the phone rang. Melissa picked it up. "It's for you, Mother." After handing the phone to Darlene, she went into the bathroom to change out of her work clothes. All the while, she rehearsed imaginary phone conversations with her father.

True to his word, Tyce arrived to pick Darlene up a few minutes to six.

"This is for you," he said, handing Melissa a large box. "You can open it after we're gone."

"Are you ready?" he asked Darlene, offering her his arm.

When the door shut behind them, Melissa opened the card attached to the box.

It's a few years late. But about time you had one.
Love,
Tyce

She read the message over and over, stumbling slightly every time she came to love.

Finally, she undid the wrapping. There in the box, nestled in tissue paper, was a stuffed teddy bear.

"Cubby," Melissa whispered as she squeezed the bear tight. "Tyce remembered."

Now she had a teddy bear; all she needed was to find her father. She looked at the phone. It seemed to have a personality of its own. Could a phone stare at you?

Melissa pulled the slip of paper from her purse. Six numbers skipped down the page. One of them might be the right one. She drew in a large breath and settled on the sofa. Should she try the most likely one first? That would be the third one down in Los Angeles. One of the numbers was just over the Oregon border, and one was clear down below San Diego. The other three were scattered across the middle of the state.

She picked up the phone and began punching in numbers.

"Hello." A soft woman's voice came across the wire.

"Hi." Melissa's stomach lurched. "I'd like to speak to Franklin Wilabee, please."

There was a long silence, then, "Who's calling?"

"This is Melissa Wilabee. I think we might be related."

"You're a little late." The voice took on a hard edge. "He died a week ago. And he didn't leave no money for relatives to fight over either."

"I'm sorry. I didn't know."

"Good-bye."

"Wait. Please. Would you tell me how old he was?"

"Why do you want to know that?"

"I'm searching for my father." Melissa rushed on with the details of the six California numbers and how she'd looked them up on the Internet. "If he was sixty-nine, he might have been my father."

"Then I guess you'll be glad to know Frank turned 101 last June." The woman's voice softened. "Hope you find your father."

Melissa was trembling when she hung up. What if she'd waited just a week too long to contact her father? A sense of urgency made her fingers fly over the next numbers.

"Hello." The male voice was deep and pleasant.

"May I speak with Franklin Wilabee?"

"This is Frank. But I'm not buying."

"I'm not a telemarketer," Melissa hastily told him. "My name's Melissa Wilabee."

"Melissa? My daughter, Melissa?"

"I think so. Did you ever live in Turner, Oregon?"

"Yes, yes! Melissa! I can't believe it. Where are you?"

In the background, Melissa heard a female voice ask, "Who is it, Frank?"

"It's my daughter. Can you believe that?"

Melissa was still on the phone two hours later when she heard the apartment door open. "Mother just arrived. I'll write. I'm so glad I found you. Bye for now."

She rose from the sofa, still clinging to the bear, as Tyce and Darlene entered. "I found him!"

"Excellent," Tyce said.

"We've been talking on the phone for the last two hours."

"How is he?" Darlene's question surprised Melissa. She hadn't known what kind of response to expect.

"He's doing well."

"I'm really happy for you," Tyce said.

"Thank you. And thanks for Cubby. I love him." She hadn't known the words would come out sounding as they did. But it was true. She loved the gift and the giver. She realized she and Tyce were gazing into each other's eyes. And she figured her grin looked as silly as his did.

"I'm glad," Tyce said.

Melissa heard the words. They translated, "Love, Tyce."

"Can you stay for a minute?" She needed to share her happiness, and she didn't think Darlene wanted to listen to the details.

"Sure." Tyce came in and shut the door. "Which number was he?"

"The fourth one on the list, but I didn't start at the top."

Melissa led him to the sofa. "Can I get you anything to drink?"

"I'm fine, thanks."

Darlene shuffled off to the bedroom without further comment.

Melissa poured out the story. "And when she said he died last week, I think I would have collapsed if I hadn't already been sitting down."

"When you reached your father, was he glad to hear from you?"

"I think he was as glad to find me as I was to find him."

"When are you going to see him?"

"I haven't figured that out yet. Maybe over Thanksgiving vacation. Beverly will be home by then. In the meantime, we're going to write and keep in touch."

"Have you let Nancy know?"

"Not yet. I just hung up as you and Mother came in the door. I still can't believe we talked for almost two hours.

There was so much we wanted to say to each other."

"I'd say this story has a happy ending."

"Happy and sad. I keep thinking of all the wasted years."

"Didn't the Apostle Paul say something about forgetting what lies behind and pressing on? I think that's where you are now. You'll spoil the joy of finding your father if you hang onto the past."

Melissa nodded. Tyce was right. But it wasn't going to be easy.

"Go ahead and call Nancy. I know she'll be waiting by the phone."

She reached for the phone and dialed the familiar numbers. "Hi, Nancy. I found him."

The squeal on the other end of the line made her move the phone away from her ear and grimace.

Tyce chuckled. "I heard that."

"Can you wait until tomorrow for all the details?"

"Do I have to?"

"Tyce is here and. . ."

"I'm gone. Talk to you tomorrow. And, Melissa, I'm so thrilled for you. Bye."

"Bye." Melissa replaced the phone and looked at Tyce. "I think I'm dreaming. This is so wonderful, how can it be true?"

"You're entitled to wonderful. But let's make sure." He reached over and pinched her arm.

"Ouch! What was that for?"

"I'm just making sure you're awake."

"I'm awake, I'm awake." She batted at his hand, which still lingered on her arm.

"Good. And you're not ready to fall asleep?"

"I'm so excited. It may take me hours to get to sleep."

"Then, in fear of being redundant, I'd like to repeat myself while I know you're wide awake."

Melissa frowned. Tyce was behaving strangely.

"I love you."

twenty

Melissa yielded to the tender kiss and embrace that followed Tyce's declaration of love. She felt the love, but even more powerful was the sense of security. His kiss vanquished a loneliness she hadn't known existed.

When he raised his head, she lost herself in the depth of his eyes. The urge to trace the outline of his lips made her fingers tremble.

"I'm thrilled you've found your father," Tyce said. "This will help fill a large void in your life. You need the kind of love only a father can give you. But I'd like to fill part of that void too."

She heard the plea in his statement and found herself nodding.

"Yes," she whispered. And just before his lips found hers again she added, "I love you too."

❧

"Well, come on, come on. Tell me all about him." Nancy pounced on Melissa before she could get her coat off. "I've waited twelve hours to hear about your contact with your father."

"It was wonderful."

"You do look radiant this morning."

Melissa smiled and hugged the memories of last night closer. She'd found two loves in one evening. She reflected that God's timing was strange. In the middle of one of her most difficult situations, He was working to bring love into her life. Fall term hadn't started with a promise of good things to come. And now it had turned into a term of love.

"Details, please," Nancy prompted.

"My father lives in California with his wife."

"He remarried? Do you have half-brothers or sisters?"

"No. They've only been married ten years. She just turned fifty-five."

"When are you going to see them?"

"I can't get away until Thanksgiving vacation. And Beverly will be home by then."

"Oh, how can you wait?"

"Some things we don't have a choice about."

"So true." Nancy got a faraway look in her eyes, and Melissa figured the questioning was over. She supposed everyone had something in their life they wished they had more control over.

"I don't suppose there's any chance your father could come here before Thanksgiving?"

"Don't think so."

❧

Melissa noticed how early the sun was setting since November started. Days were slipping by fast, and she'd marked each one off on her calendar. The day after phoning her father, she'd marked the November date when she could head to California. As she passed the calendar hanging on the kitchen wall, she felt a rush of anticipation.

Tyce was coming over this evening for dinner, and she checked the pork chops in the oven. The breading on top was browning nicely.

The outside buzzer sounded, and she reached for the release button.

"Wow! Smells good in here." Tyce took off his coat and followed Melissa into the kitchen. He planted a solid kiss on her lips before asking, "Anything I can do to help?"

"You can set the butter and salt and pepper on the table."

"Where's Darlene?"

"She's in the bedroom. Ever since I picked her up from the senior center she's been acting strangely."

"How do you mean?"

"I guess depressed would describe it best."

"Did you ask about her mood?"

"She just said nothing's wrong."

"Think she'd talk to me?"

"I'm sure you have a better chance of finding out than I do." She tried hard not to sound bitter.

Tyce came and gave her a hug. "I'll go tap on the door and see what's up."

"Okay. Dinner's about ready."

She watched him cross the room. He moved with a light step for such a big man, like the big cats. He knocked softly on the bedroom door. "Darlene, it's Tyce. May I come in?"

Melissa didn't hear an answer but saw Tyce turn the knob and go in. For a moment she stood by the stove with indecision. Then she gave a quick look in the oven and turned the burner low under the boiling potatoes. She was drawn to the bedroom doorway like metal filings to a magnet, eavesdropping with hardly a twinge of her conscience.

"How are you doing, Darlene?"

"Not too good."

"Sorry to hear that. Anything I can do?"

"Do you have a spare brain to loan?"

Melissa heard Tyce chuckle and couldn't resist the urge to peek around the doorframe. Darlene sat on the edge of the bed, and Tyce stood in front of her. He bent down on one knee, putting him closer to her eye level.

"Having trouble with the one you've got?"

Darlene nodded.

"Did something happen today?"

She nodded again. A tear escaped and rolled down her wrinkled cheek. "I forgot how."

Melissa held her breath and strained to hear every word.

Tyce picked up one of Darlene's hands, which lay limp in her lap.

"Now everyone knows." Her head bobbed up and down

like Petey pecking at his feeder.

Melissa waited for Tyce's words of comfort, but he remained silent as he stroked the hand in his grasp.

Darlene looked up with a belligerent jut to her lower lip. "I don't mind getting lost. Someone always comes and finds me. But I hate not remembering which card to play!"

Melissa had taken some comfort in thinking Darlene didn't know her mind was failing, that she didn't remember wandering off and having the police find her. That comfort was shattered. Darlene was suffering over her dementia as much as Melissa was. Maybe more.

"What is she going to do with me?" Darlene's frightened whisper brought tears to Melissa's eyes. "She and Franklin will have me put away for what I've done."

The timer on the stove went off, indicating the chops were done. Petey cocked his head at the sound and yelled, "Not now. Not now."

You're right about that, bird. Melissa was torn between shutting off the irritating alarm or staying to hear what Tyce would say.

"Sounds like dinner is ready."

Melissa realized Tyce was ignoring Darlene's last statement. But she couldn't ignore the pain she heard in her mother's voice.

Melissa stepped into the bedroom. "No, Mother. No one is going to put you away." She settled on the edge of the bed and took Darlene's other hand. "You must have been very angry at Dad to keep me from getting in contact with him."

Darlene glanced sideways at Melissa but didn't say anything.

"Thank you for not throwing the letters away." Dad's letters were her link to the past. Now Melissa realized it was the future that frightened Darlene.

"Mother, we'll talk about arrangements for you when Beverly gets home."

There was still a wary look on Darlene's face as she turned to

Melissa. Melissa didn't know why, but it was suddenly important that Darlene not fear the future. "Honest. I'm too happy to have found Dad to want to take revenge. Besides, aren't you enjoying being with the folks down at the senior center?"

Darlene nodded. "Usually."

"Well, we'll just have to find someplace nice like that where you can make new friends, and they can give you the help you need when you have trouble with your memory."

"An old folks home." Darlene's statement was heavy with depression. "Just somewhere to get me out of your way."

"No, Mother. You are not in my way." Despite all that had happened, Melissa believed it was true. "I never had a chance to really get to know Dad. I've wanted that for a long time. Now I realize I've never understood you either. Maybe we can work at getting to know each other better."

"Hey, is that the buzzer on the stove I still hear?" Tyce asked.

"Oh, the chops!" Melissa dashed from the room.

"May I help you put your shoes on?" Tyce asked Darlene, picking up a black oxford from the floor. "Then we'll go eat."

Over dinner, Tyce entertained the two women with stories of his soccer years. "I missed three shots in a row and figured the coach would sack me. I can't remember ever having such a bad day on the field since I was in little league. But Coach said, 'It happens sometimes. Try again tomorrow.' That was it. He didn't bawl me out or make me do extra laps. I've always remembered that. It made more of an impression than any of the times he yelled at me."

They cleared the dishes, and Darlene retreated to her room. Petey took up his "Yankee Doodle" refrain. He sang the first seven notes over and over.

"Okay, Petey." Melissa grabbed the black cloth. "Good night," she said, throwing the cover over the cage.

Melissa came back and nestled into the spot on the sofa next to Tyce. "Sometimes I feel like Petey, all caged up."

"Petey's stuck with a caged life; you have choices."

"But choices mean making decisions."

"That's true. But making decisions isn't all bad. Especially if you have someone to help you along the way." Tyce reached into his jacket pocket and placed a jeweler's box in Melissa's hand.

"I'm applying for the position."

A Letter To Our Readers

Dear Reader:

In order that we might better contribute to your reading enjoyment, we would appreciate your taking a few minutes to respond to the following questions. We welcome your comments and read each form and letter we receive. When completed, please return to the following:

Fiction Editor
Heartsong Presents
PO Box 719
Uhrichsville, Ohio 44683

1. Did you enjoy reading *Term of Love* by Myrtlemay Pittman Crane?

   ❑ Very much! I would like to see more books by this author!
   ❑ Moderately. I would have enjoyed it more if

   _____
   _____
   _____

2. Are you a member of **Heartsong Presents**? ❑ Yes ❑ No
   If no, where did you purchase this book? _____
   _____

3. How would you rate, on a scale from 1 (poor) to 5 (superior), the cover design? _____

4. On a scale from 1 (poor) to 10 (superior), please rate the following elements.

   ____ Heroine   ____ Plot
   ____ Hero   ____ Inspirational theme
   ____ Setting   ____ Secondary characters

5. These characters were special because?_____

_____

_____

6. How has this book inspired your life?_____

_____

_____

7. What settings would you like to see covered in future **Heartsong Presents** books? _____

_____

_____

8. What are some inspirational themes you would like to see treated in future books? _____

_____

_____

9. Would you be interested in reading other **Heartsong Presents** titles? ❏ Yes ❏ No

10. Please check your age range:
   ❏ Under 18   ❏ 18-24
   ❏ 25-34   ❏ 35-45
   ❏ 46-55   ❏ Over 55

Name_____

Occupation _____

Address _____

City_____ State_____ Zip_____

Minnesota

*I*n 1877, the citizens of Chippewa Falls, Minnesota, are recovering from the devastation of a five-year grasshopper infestation. Throughout the years that follow, countless hardships, trials, and life-threatening dangers will plague the settlers as they struggle for survival amidst the harsh environs and crude conditions of the state's southwest plains. Yet love always prevails.

Historical, paperback, 480 pages, 5 ³/₁₆" x 8"

❤ ❤ ❤ ❤ ❤ ❤ ❤ ❤ ❤ ❤ ❤ ❤ ❤ ❤ ❤

❤ ❤ ❤ ❤ ❤ ❤ ❤ ❤ ❤ ❤ ❤ ❤ ❤ ❤ ❤

Presents

Great Inspirational Romance at a Great Price!

Heartsong Presents books are inspirational romances in contemporary and historical settings, designed to give you an enjoyable, spirit-lifting reading experience. You can choose wonderfully written titles from some of today's best authors like Hannah Alexander, Andrea Boeshaar, Yvonne Lehman, Tracie Peterson, and many others.

When ordering quantities less than twelve, above titles are $3.25 each.
Not all titles may be available at time of order.